"You're not watching the meteors," Garrett said.

"Huh?" she asked as she glanced over at him.

He pointed toward the sky, and that was when she realized she must have been staring out into the darkness of the surrounding range land. "Guess I'm more tired than I thought."

"You sure that's it?"

She fixed her gaze on her cast, cursing it and how it prevented her from making a hasty exit from her current situation.

"Yeah." She knew her answer sounded weak and not entirely truthful, but it was the best she could muster. Sitting so close to Garrett made it hard for her to think.

Garrett slid off the tailgate. "I'll take you back in."

She reached out and grabbed his arm. "No, it's okay. We can wait until it's over."

He captured and held her gaze. "You said you're tired."

She fought the burning need to lower her gaze to that amazing chest of his. "I'll sleep later. This meteor shower doesn't come around very often."

He stared at her in a way that made her feel as if he was picking through the layers of her brain. And then she watched as his eyes lowered for a moment to her lips. How she wished she could lean forward, invite him to do more than just look.

The Heart of a Cowboy

TRISH MILBURN

First published in Great Britain 2015
by Mills & Boon, an imprint of Harlequin (UK) Limited,
Large Print edition 2015
Eton House, 18-24 Paradise Road,
Richmond, Surrey, TW9 1SR

ISBN: 978-0-263-26001-4

Printed and bound in Great Britain
by CPI Antony Rowe, Chippenham, Wiltshire

TRISH MILBURN

writes contemporary romance for the Mills & Boon® Cherish™ line and paranormal romance for the Mills & Boon® Nocturne series. She's a two-time Golden Heart® Award winner, a fan of walks in the woods and road trips, and a big geek girl, including being a dedicated Whovian and Browncoat. And from her earliest memories, she's been a fan of Westerns, be they historical or contemporary. There's nothing quite like a cowboy hero.

To everyone who has ever found the courage to face adversity head-on or to accept a happy ending when it came your way. Sometimes accepting the latter is every bit as hard as accepting the former.

Chapter One

The new colt marshaled his strength and pushed up onto his long, spindly legs for the first time, drawing a smile from Natalie Todd. She watched as the little guy steadied himself on legs spread wide then as his dam groomed him. A couple of wobbly steps brought the newborn close enough to his mother to nurse. No matter how many horses Natalie helped into the world, the wonder never faded.

"Hard to believe they were in distress only an hour ago," Jacob Hartwell said as he came to stand beside her.

"Maybe Mama here just wanted some female company."

Jacob laughed a little. "Maybe. She certainly doesn't have a lot around here."

Steven Hartwell, patriarch of the Hartwell ranching family, was a widower, and his two sons, Steven Jr. and Jacob, were still single. Even though Jacob flirted with her a little every time she came out to the ranch, she knew it was harmless and not at all serious.

"Well, it looks like you have a handsome little fella to add to your testosterone ranch."

"You could always marry me and bring some female beauty to the place."

Natalie rolled her eyes and stepped back from the stall. "See ya around, Jacob."

"Thanks again, Doc."

She threw him a wave as she turned and headed out of the barn into the deep cover of night. As she strode toward her truck, she considered just curling up in the seat and catching a quick nap. She'd had a long day at the clinic and then because she was the vet on call tonight, her phone had rung about fifteen minutes after she'd fallen asleep.

When she dragged herself into the driver's seat, however, her thoughts drifted to her comfortable bed. What was another half hour's drive back to her apartment? Hopefully there wouldn't be any more equine or bovine emergencies tonight. At least the Hartwells' ranch was closer to her place south of Wichita than a lot of other ranches the clinic serviced.

She started the engine and headed toward the highway. Once she got away from the ranch, the landscape darkened around her. With no moon and some cloud cover, the southern Kansas landscape was pitch-black. It took ten minutes of driving before she began to see the glow of Wichita's lights to the north. Only a few minutes and a quick shower more and she'd be curling back into her bed.

Her phone rang on the seat beside her, eliciting a groan and, yes, maybe even a whimper. She slowed, thankful there wasn't any traffic, and glanced at the phone. Her heart gave a painful thud when she saw it was her mom calling. Knowing it wasn't going to be a happy conversation, she pulled off the road. Her hand shook as she picked up the phone and answered.

"Hi, Mom."

"Did I wake you?" Her mother's voice sounded tired, but then Natalie couldn't really remember a time when her mom wasn't tired.

"No. Actually, I'm driving back from delivering a foal." When her mom didn't say anything in response, Natalie knew for certain why her mother had called. "It's time, isn't it?"

"Yes." Now her mom's voice sounded as if it was laced with tears.

"I'll get there as fast as I can."

"Be safe, okay? I don't want you to have a wreck."

"I'll be careful."

But even though Natalie knew that her father's time was ticking away, she didn't speed. Though it made no sense, some part of her believed if she drew out how long it took her to arrive at her parents' house in Wichita, the longer her dad would have. But that was cruel because he was suffering, had been suffering for a long time. That's what a lifetime of drinking brought a person, a painful death via liver failure.

Pain of a different kind punched her right in her middle, the realization that probably before the night was through her dad would be gone forever. She bit her bottom lip and pressed down harder on the accelerator.

Twenty minutes later, she pulled up in front of

her parents' small home, the one she'd helped them buy because they never would have been able to purchase one on their own. She cut the engine but didn't get out of the truck. Instead, she stared at her mom's older-model car sitting in the carport. Behind it sat a small SUV belonging to her sister Allison, who'd driven down the day before from Kansas City, bringing their youngest sister, Renee, with her. Her entire family was inside the little blond-brick home, sitting around waiting for her father to die.

She gripped the steering wheel, fighting the visceral need to drive away, as far and as fast as she could. Even though she'd known this moment was coming for months, she still wasn't ready. It wasn't as if she had a perfect relationship with her dad, but he was still her dad and she loved him, despite everything. She wanted to be angry that he'd done this to himself, that his drinking had made his wife's and daughters' lives much more difficult than they should have been. But what was the use of being angry now? It wasn't going to change the outcome.

With a deep, shaky breath, she opened the truck door and slipped out onto the quiet street. Almost every light in every house was dark, except for those of her parents and Jackie Kincaid across the street, the neighborhood gossip to beat all neighborhood gossips. Natalie resisted the evil urge to find the nearest paintball gun and cover Jackie's big picture window with globs of paint. Instead, she forced herself to walk toward her parents' front door.

She didn't knock, instead slipping quietly into the living room to find Renee sitting there alone, reading a copy of some French magazine she'd obviously brought with her from Paris. Natalie had the unkind thought that Renee might have brought the magazine solely as an outward symbol of just how far away she'd gone from Wichita and their family. Part of Natalie couldn't blame her for leaving, but now wasn't the time to bring it up. Natalie kept those thoughts to herself as her sister looked up and smiled at her.

"Hey, Nat." Renee jumped up and wrapped Natalie in a hug.

Needing that hug more than she cared to admit, Natalie held her baby sister a little longer than Renee probably expected, then continued to hold on to her upper arms as she took in how different her sister looked.

"I like the new haircut," she said as she finally released her sister.

Renee ran a hand over the chic bob. "Thanks."

As Natalie examined Renee from head to toe, she realized that her sister looked more European than Midwestern. An odd sense of loss settled in Natalie's heart despite the fact that Renee had been living in France for five years.

Natalie glanced toward the hallway that led to the bedrooms. "How's he doing?"

"Dreadful."

Natalie jerked as if she'd been slapped.

Renee softened her expression. "Sorry. I'm too blunt sometimes."

"I know you probably don't want to be here, but thanks for coming."

Renee shrugged. "I'm not totally without feeling. There's a part of me that loves him because he's my dad, even though he wasn't worth much."

"Renee." Natalie knew she sounded like the scolding older sister, but she couldn't help it even though there was some truth in her sister's words.

"Tell me I'm wrong."

Natalie couldn't. Their dad's drinking had

led to him not being able to keep a job, to their mom working two jobs to support their family of five. He hadn't been mean, or violent, but his inability to conquer whatever demons that led him to drink had caused his family a lot of hardship.

Not wanting to focus on the past, Natalie instead took a fortifying breath and headed toward her parents' bedroom. The mingling scents of cleansers and sickness assaulted her as she entered the bedroom, and it took all her effort not to let the way her stomach turned show on her face.

Allison was the first to notice her and gave her a tired smile. Her sister reached across the bed and gently touched her mom's hand and nodded toward Natalie.

Her mom stood on legs that looked as shaky as the newborn colt's and wrapped Natalie in her arms. "I'm glad you made it safely."

Natalie was struck by just how thin her mother felt and wondered if she hadn't been eating properly.

"There's my other girl."

Natalie looked toward the sound of her father's thin, labored voice. As unkind as it was to think it, Renee was right. Bill Todd did look dreadful with jaundiced skin and eyes, cracked lips and swelling in his abdomen that was obvious even under the blanket covering him. He'd never been a big, strapping man, but now he honestly looked like the death he was facing.

Her mom stepped back, indicating that Natalie should take the dining room chair that sat next to the bed. Natalie wondered how many hours her mother had sat in that uncomfortable chair at her husband's side, watching him slip away more with each passing minute.

"Hey, Dad." Somehow she managed to force

some chipper light into her voice as she sat and placed her hand over his gnarled one.

He tried to squeeze her hand but obviously didn't have the strength to do so. Sadness swept over her, not so much that his life was ending but that so much of it had been wasted. All the times he'd made her mad, embarrassed her, caused her to question why she hadn't been born into another family tumbled through her mind. It all could have been so different if he hadn't been trapped in an unhealthy relationship with alcohol.

"I'd like to talk to Natalie alone." He took a shallow breath, as if only a small portion of his lungs remained functional.

Natalie tried to figure out why he'd want her mother and Allison to leave the room, but then she caught a glance between her parents, an understanding of some sort. What was going on?

Her mom ushered an equally confused Allison from the room and closed the door behind them. When Natalie looked back at her dad, his eyes were closed, and for a split second she thought he was gone. But then she saw the faint movement of his chest.

"Do you remember when I took you fishing the first time?"

Her forehead wrinkled at the out-of-nowhere question, and she wondered if his mind was going before his body. When he opened his eyes and focused on her, she realized she hadn't answered him.

"Yeah. The first and only, if I recall."

The edges of his mouth lifted in a weak smile, and she forced one in return though she'd never felt less like smiling.

"You always did love animals of all kinds, couldn't stand to see them hurt," he said. "I can still see the tears in your eyes when you realized the hook was stuck in the fish's mouth."

Even though she'd been sad at the time, as she looked back it was one of her favorite memories of her dad. They'd still lived in Texas then, and that day he'd seemed to be totally sober, the kind of dad she'd always wanted. Though it'd been many years since that day, she remembered the hope that had surged within her. Sometimes hope was cruel when it led you down a path toward even more hurt.

His smile faded away, and she wasn't sure if it was because it took too much energy to maintain or a darker thought had shoved aside the happy memory.

Despite everything, she searched for a way to make him smile again. "I remember we sat beside the lake and had chicken-salad sandwiches and bread-and-butter pickles from the Primrose Café."

The barest hint of a smile tugged at his lips.

"I can't believe you remember all those details. You were so small."

She'd liked living in Blue Falls and the fun she'd had with her best friend, Chloe. But she also remembered how her heart had broken when her dad said they had to move to Kansas. She'd watched the lights of Blue Falls fade away as she stared through the back window of their old Buick sedan, fat tears streaming down her face.

Her father turned his hand so that he could hold hers. "I'm sorry I wasn't the father you and your sisters should have had. I wanted to be, but…" He shook his head on his pillow. "There's no excuse."

She wanted to tell him it was okay, to let him be able to slip into the next life knowing he was forgiven. But the words got stuck in her throat, and all she could manage was to squeeze his hand. He looked so haunted, more so than she'd ever seen him.

"What was it that made you drink so much, Dad?" She'd asked before, many times, but he'd never had an answer. The intensity of her need to know felt as if it was burning a hole inside her. This time, when his eyes met hers, she could tell he was finally going to tell her. Suddenly, she was scared to know the truth. Had it been better all along not knowing?

No, she needed this answer, whether or not it proved satisfying.

"There was a reason we left Texas. I…I was in an accident." He paused, and she wondered if he was reconsidering telling her the truth. "I hit someone, and then I ran."

"You were in a hit-and-run?" For some reason, it took a moment for her to realize he'd fled because he was driving drunk, that he could have ended up in jail.

"Yes. I hit another car. I stopped to check on the driver, but…there was nothing I could do."

Natalie's stomach churned. Surely he wasn't saying what it seemed, that he'd… "Dad, no."

"I knew the moment I saw her that she was dead."

Oh, God, this couldn't be happening. Without thinking, she slipped her hand out of her father's grasp. "You're confused, not remembering things correctly." That was a symptom of late-stage liver failure, right? This couldn't be a horrible deathbed confession.

"I wish that was true." He shifted his eyes to stare at the ceiling, and she got the impression it was so he wouldn't cry. "But the truth is that your father is worse than you ever realized. I killed someone and I never owned up to it, not even when I realized who I'd hit."

"You knew her?" Her question came out as a strangled whisper. But in the next breath, the true horror of his confession slammed into her. "No. Please tell me you're not saying what I think you are."

His bottom lip trembled and he lost the war against his tears. "It was Karen Brody."

Natalie stood so quickly that she knocked the chair over and nearly followed it to the floor. Karen Brody, Chloe's mom, the woman who had been like a second mother to Natalie. As if the mere mention of her name pulled a sense memory from Natalie's mind, she suddenly smelled fresh sugar cookies straight from Karen's oven.

She paced across the room, hoping that she was having a nightmare and the movement would make her wake up. But when she finally stopped and looked at her dad, any hope that she was dreaming disappeared like water down a drain.

For what felt like hours, she simply stood

searching for something to say. But what did you say when your father admitted he'd killed your best friend's mother?

"Mom and I went to her funeral. Chloe clung to me and cried so hard I thought she would fall to pieces." She shook her head slowly, her heart breaking in so many ways she couldn't count them all. "Why didn't you come forward?"

"Because I was scared, a coward. And we thought they'd take you away from us."

It took a few beats for Natalie to process all the information coming toward her like poison-tipped arrows. "We?" Then the way her parents had exchanged that glance a few minutes before caused a lump to form in her throat. "Mom knew? Oh, my God. She knew and she still walked into that funeral home and hugged Karen's kids."

Her stomach churned so violently she was afraid she was going to vomit.

"We were so scared. We couldn't lose you and your sisters."

"Chloe, Owen and Garrett lost their mother!"

A sob shook her father's failing body, and she did her best to rein in her anger.

"If I could go back and do things differently, I would," he said, his breath growing more labored. "I'd have gone to prison, but maybe you all would have been better off without me."

Despite the anger and horror nearly choking her, the pure, unadulterated pain and sorrow she heard in his voice made her feel a sliver of compassion for him. This then was the reason he drank so much more after they moved to Kansas, to try to forget that he'd ended someone's life. To drown the guilt.

She wanted to set fire to every alcoholic beverage in the world and wipe the knowledge of how to make them from the memories of mankind.

"I want to make it right, but I need you to help me do that," he said.

Suddenly so weak she felt as if she might collapse in a heap, she righted the overturned chair with a shaking hand and sank onto the seat again. "There's no way to make this right, Dad. What's done is done."

Even if they told the cops now, most likely they wouldn't even arrive until after her father had passed from this earth. Honestly, by the look of him, she was stunned he'd found the strength to voice his confession.

"I need for you to tell the Brodys the truth, tell them how very sorry I am. Your mother can't do it because they might come after her for knowing."

She shook her head, unable to believe what he was asking her to do. "I can't. It'll just reopen all the old wounds. It won't bring Karen back."

"But they'll have the answer to the question they've never been able to find."

But would that be worse than never knowing?

Natalie dropped her head into her hands, feeling as if the entirety of her insides were being scalded raw. Gradually, the fact that her dad's breathing was becoming even more labored registered, and she looked up to see tears still streaking out of his tired eyes. Though it was impossible, he seemed even smaller than when she'd walked into the room.

Yes, she was angrier than she ever remembered being, but could she let her dad die without promising him that she'd fulfill his dying wish? She knew it wasn't fair of him to ask it of her, and he likely knew it, too. But he'd carried the guilt with him for so long, and it had obviously eaten away at him every bit as much as the alcohol, probably more.

Though she had no idea how she would be

able to face the Brodys with such a horrible truth, she found herself unable to let her father slip from the world with his heart so unbearably heavy.

"I'll tell them." She'd figure out the how later.

The relief came off her father like a wave, and something felt profoundly right about what she'd just given him. In her entire life, she'd never witnessed such a deep desire to make amends.

Evidently no longer able to lift his hand, he pointed only one finger toward his nightstand. "There's a letter for them."

Natalie opened the drawer to find an envelope addressed to the Brody family in his distinctive scrawl. She didn't have to look inside to know that it was his confession, the cleansing of his conscience before he died. She wondered how long the letter had occupied the drawer. He would have had to pen it some time ago since there was no way he could have managed it in recent days.

Though the envelope and the paper inside were no heavier than any other, she felt as if she held a terrible weight in her hand. She took a moment to inhale slowly then let the breath back out, fighting the dizziness that had decided to arrive to keep her nausea company. She tried to imagine what it must have been like to keep such a horrible secret for more than two decades, and the very idea threatened to make her even more ill. But at least her father hadn't taken the truth to his grave.

"I think it's…" Her words faded away as she looked up at her dad. His last tears were still drying on his grizzled cheeks as the first of hers fell.

No matter what he'd done, he was her dad and she loved him.

And now he was gone.

The sadness of his loss joined with the terrible weight of his confession, and she suddenly and desperately needed a breath of fresh air that didn't smell like death and regret. She stood and walked slowly from the room, only dimly aware of her mother and sisters speaking to her as she headed for the front door.

As soon as she stepped outside and the clean air enveloped her, she stumbled, reminding her yet again of the colt's shaky legs. The universe had a strange way of ensuring balance, constantly bringing a new life into the world at the same time it took another out.

As she looked up at the sky, she realized the clouds had given way to a blanket of stars. She gripped one of the porch supports as she thought about how the Brodys could be looking up at those same stars totally unaware that she'd just promised to bring them an answer they might no longer want.

Chapter Two

Garrett Brody still thought there was a high likelihood he would wake up any minute and realize he'd been dreaming. After all, the fact that he was at his younger brother's wedding didn't compute. Owen was not the getting-hitched-and-settling-down type. At least he hadn't been until Linnea Holland had arrived at their family's ranch with a heart broken in the worst possible way when she discovered her fiancé was already married. Somehow, his baby brother had helped Linnea heal, and her presence had convinced Owen that settling down with one woman was what he'd been searching for all along.

As Garrett watched the newlyweds dance with huge smiles on their faces, he had to admit he'd never seen his brother look so genuinely happy.

"Pretty sure hell has finally frozen over."

Garrett glanced over to where Greg Bozeman, the ace mechanic of Blue Falls, was standing with a cup of punch. "No, that's reserved for when you tie the knot."

"Bite your tongue, man."

Garrett chuckled as he watched Greg scan the room full of wedding guests, no doubt scoping out the single ladies. Speaking of, Garrett spotted Jenna Marks looking his direction. Before she got it in her head to walk his way, he nudged Greg and indicated he should go ask Jenna to dance.

"Sure you don't want to reserve her for yourself?"

"Yep." And to add a little extra buffer, he headed toward where his sister and her husband, Wyatt, were spinning around the dance floor to a Luke Bryan song.

He tapped Wyatt's shoulder. "Mind if I cut in?"

"Be my guest. Let your sister step on your toes for a bit."

Chloe huffed and swatted her husband's arm. "It was only once and I was trying to avoid bumping into Verona."

"Sure," Wyatt said before planting a quick kiss on his wife's cheek.

She playfully pushed him away. "Don't be surprised when I make you sleep on the porch."

Wyatt just grinned as he took a step back, well aware that Chloe's threat was empty.

Those two were every bit as in love as Owen and Linnea.

A sense of being the odd man out settled on Garrett. Blue Falls residents of the betting persuasion would have likely given him the best odds of settling down and starting a family first among his siblings, but things just hadn't worked out that way. He went out now and then, but he'd never met a woman with whom he felt he could be happy spending the rest of his life.

"So, what brings you to the dance floor, big brother?"

"I need a reason to dance with my sister at our brother's wedding?"

She lifted an eyebrow, but he didn't take the bait. Instead, he led her into a dance as a new song began. They moved past their youngest sibling just as Owen dipped Linnea backward, causing the blushing bride to laugh and cling to Owen's arms as if he might drop her on the floor. Garrett knew better. Owen wouldn't do anything to hurt Linnea. In fact, he'd take a bullet for her without a moment's hesitation. Garrett wondered what that was like, to be that in love with another person.

"You okay?"

He shifted his attention back to Chloe. "Yeah."

She didn't appear to believe him, and for a moment the look in her eyes reminded him of their mother. Even though he'd spent more of his life without his mom than with, he could still remember the way she'd look at him if she suspected he wasn't telling the truth. It was as if she could actually see the lie forming in his mind.

Chloe glanced over at Owen and Linnea, now firmly locked in a close embrace despite the fast-paced song. "You know you're next."

Garrett snorted. "That's unlikely when all the eligible possibilities keep getting snapped up."

"There are plenty of available women around, and you know it. Take Jenna Marks, for example."

It wasn't any secret that the nurse at the clinic where his sister worked as a doctor was interested in him. But the feeling wasn't mutual. Jenna was nice enough, and pretty, but he felt no real attraction to her. He'd even wondered if something was fried in his brain, but he couldn't force an affection that wasn't there.

"Small problem," he said when he noticed Chloe was still waiting for some type of response. "We already tried going on a date, and the two of us had about as much connection as a cow and a chicken."

Chloe sighed. "If Jenna isn't the type of woman you're looking for, then who is?"

"Who said I'm looking?"

"No one, but I'm just that smart."

"Cocky, too."

Chloe grinned wide, as if she was pleased with herself.

"Have you joined the Verona Charles match-making bandwagon?" Verona was the aunt of their friend Elissa and had taken it upon herself to pair up any unattached person who crossed her path. And with each successful pairing, including his two siblings, she grew even more ambitious. It didn't matter if she was a big part of two people getting together or simply contributed a gentle nudge, she seemed to take great pleasure in seeing Blue Falls fill up with happily-ever-afters. He imagined a room of her house filled with a big dry-erase board akin to a basketball playoff bracket filled with the names of all the local singles.

"Not officially," Chloe said. "But I want to see you happy."

"I wasn't aware I appear unhappy."

"It's not that you seem sad, but there's something missing."

He didn't want to acknowledge that she'd hit the nail on the head, partially because he'd nearly convinced himself that he was okay with his life as it was. Honestly, how many people grew up to live their lives exactly as they imagined them when they were younger?

As the eldest of the Brody children, he'd always assumed he'd follow in his father's footsteps running the cattle ranch, getting married and having children of his own. As the years passed and none of his dates led to anything even approaching what his father had with his mom before her death, Garrett had gradually accepted that perhaps the ranching aspect was the only part of his imagined future that would come to fruition. After all, the dating pool wasn't endless in a town the size of Blue Falls.

And he sure as hell wasn't going to resort to some online dating site. They worked fine for some people, but he damn near broke out in hives just thinking about it.

"You worry too much," he finally said. "If it's meant to happen, it will."

And if it wasn't, he'd keep his focus on ranching, making sure that the Brody spread stayed out of the red. Ranching was a tough way of life, but he couldn't imagine doing anything else. And that didn't always appeal to women. Part of him could understand. Unless ranching ran in your blood, who would want to volunteer for a life where a drought or an illness in the herd could wipe you out?

They'd very nearly lost the ranch once in those dark days after his mother's death, when his father had been consumed by grief and they'd been slammed with a severe drought nearly at the same time. The stress of losing the love of his life and then almost losing his means of supporting his children had been palpable. Garrett was determined that his father would never be that close to the mental or financial breaking point ever again. Not to mention, if Garrett ever did marry, he wanted the ranch to be a successful enterprise he could hand down to his children as well as any nieces and nephews who might come along.

"You'll find someone," Chloe said as he guided her around Liam and India Parrish, yet another couple Verona had been instrumental in pairing up. "I have faith."

She might but Garrett wasn't so sure. Considering he was already thirty-two, that possibility didn't look too good.

As the party started winding down a few minutes later, he leaned over to give his sister a kiss on the cheek.

"I'm going to head out. Have fun on your

trip." Since Chloe and Wyatt had yet to go on their own honeymoon, they were going on the same Caribbean cruise as Owen and Linnea.

"Thanks. I'll be sure to bring you some tacky, touristy T-shirt."

He laughed a little. "I've been needing a new grease rag for when I work on the trucks."

She gave him an exasperated look. "Oh, go on before I tell Verona that you're dying to find a wife as soon as possible."

Garrett handed her off to Wyatt. "Your wife is evil."

"I know, but she's cute."

He left one starry-eyed couple only to walk toward another, maneuvering through the crowd to Owen and Linnea. He playfully punched Owen in the shoulder as he had countless times before.

"I'd tell you to have a good trip, but I doubt there's a need."

Owen grinned. "I'm already there in my mind."

Not wanting to think about what images were swirling through his brother's head, Garrett pulled Linnea into a hug. "Don't let my brother fall off the boat."

Linnea smiled as she stepped back from him. "Oh, I plan to have him wear a life jacket anytime he leaves the cabin."

Their dad, who was standing nearby, momentarily choked on the bite of cake he'd just taken. Garrett had to admit the image of his brother sitting down to a fancy dinner in the ship's dining room with a big orange life jacket around his neck was pretty darn funny.

After making his final goodbyes, he made his way outside. The lack of sound as he stood on the edge of the Wildflower Inn's parking lot made him realize just how noisy it had been inside. For the first time in several hours, he felt as if he could truly breathe. He'd rather be alone out in the middle of the ranch than in the midst of that many chattering people.

Even so, as he got into his truck and drove off the lot, the idea of going home to an empty house didn't appeal to him. Maybe he'd run down to the Blue Falls Music Hall and see who was playing tonight. If he was lucky, being in the familiar, less formal environs would help him forget how the seed of loneliness inside him had evidently been watered and fed a healthy dose of fertilizer.

NATALIE BARELY HAD time to pull over on the side of the country road and get out of the car before throwing up what little she'd been able to eat since leaving Wichita that morning. The closer she'd gotten to Texas, the more ill she'd felt. When she'd driven through Blue Falls a few minutes before, her out-of-control nerves had her seriously considering making a U-turn and driving back to Kansas. She'd lost count of how many times she'd gone back and forth in her mind about if she could go through with telling the Brodys the truth, whether she should.

Her stomach tightened again as she held on to the bumper of the truck and dry heaved. Only through some deeply buried force of will did she bring her stomach into submission. She stood shaking for a couple more minutes until she was fairly certain her insides wouldn't stage another revolt. Then she slowly walked back to the driver's door, which was standing wide open, and reached inside for a bottle of water. She washed out her mouth and spit onto the edge of the asphalt before digging in her luggage for mouthwash. She followed a full minty rinse with a few more swishes of water.

After shoving the bottle of mouthwash back into the bag, she leaned against the side of the truck and took several slow, deep breaths. She lifted her gaze to the huge expanse of dark sky peppered with stars and a sliver of moon. A rush of anger bubbled up inside her that her father had put her in this position, puking on the side of a road she barely remembered from her childhood, mere minutes away from dropping a bomb in the middle of the Brodys' lives.

She didn't have to do this.

Yes, she did. Never in her life had she failed to keep a promise. Even before she consciously knew what she was doing, something inside her had decided that she would be the total opposite of her dad in that regard. He'd made so many promises—to quit drinking, to get another job and keep it this time, to earn enough so they could take a real family vacation that wasn't a weekend of tent camping at the state park a half hour from their house.

Natalie closed her eyes as she rested her head

back against the cool metal of the truck. No matter how many times her father had disappointed her, there was one promise he'd kept. To always love her, Allison and Renee with all his heart. If she'd ever doubted that love, that doubt would have been erased by the look in his tired eyes as he'd wept mere moments before dying. He knew, soul deep, that he'd let them all down repeatedly. She'd seen the fervent wish that he'd been a better father, a better husband, a better man.

That look and her own love for him in spite of everything was why she was here in the middle of Texas. Since the night her father had asked her to deliver his apology, she'd not gotten a full night of sleep, had been able to eat only enough to keep functioning as she helped her mother deal with the funeral arrangements and laying her dad to rest. The anxiety had built over the past week until she knew she had to get this trip over with so she could begin to live normally again.

She filled her lungs with another deep breath and tried to steady her nerves as she slid back into the driver's seat. Exhaustion weighed down every cell in her body as she pulled onto the road. She knew she should wait until the next day to go see the Brodys, to try to get some sleep first, but if she had to wait another day to divulge her father's secret, she thought she might explode.

Her GPS guided her the rest of the way to the Brody ranch. When she turned into the gravel drive, she hit the brakes. She'd crossed this point so many times when she'd been a kid, and happy memories were attached to each visit here. But all of those memories were about to be poisoned by the purpose for her return.

She pressed her hand to her forehead, feeling the warm flush invading her skin. With a shake of her head, she gradually released the brake and drove the rest of the way up to the house. As her lights cut across the front, revealing two basset hounds lying at the top of the steps, she remembered sitting on those same steps with Chloe playing Go Fish as Chloe's mom sat in the rocking chair shucking corn from her garden.

But even knowing that she had to get the revelation over with, she still sat in the truck for a couple of minutes after parking and cutting the engine. She'd spent more than nine hours on the road. That should have been enough time to prep herself. Still, as she looked toward the front door she'd walked through countless times, she had to corral every speck of willpower she possessed to finally slip out of the truck.

Her feet moved slowly, the sound of her shoes on the walkway magnified by her anxiety. She found she barely had the strength to climb the steps, pausing halfway up them to pet the two hounds. When they sniffed then licked her hand, a wholly unexpected smile lifted her lips. It faded quickly when she pushed herself up the rest of the steps.

When she stood in front of the door, she had to take a few moments to catch her breath. It wasn't too late. She could still turn around, leave, not drag the painful past back into the Brodys' lives. But then she thought of her father, of how he'd suffered because he'd been weak. So that he could truly rest, she had to be strong for him and hope that her childhood best friend didn't hate her for it.

She lifted her hand and knocked on the front door. The wait for someone to answer grew to an excruciating length. When no one appeared, she knocked again, harder this time. Still no answer, or in response to a third even louder knocking.

Natalie leaned her head against the door, suddenly so tired she could barely stand. She couldn't decide if she wanted to cry that the inevitable was being drawn out even more, or if she was thankful for the temporary reprieve. She considered sitting in one of the chairs on the porch to wait for the Brodys to return home, but she was more likely than not to fall asleep there. And it only added to her sadness that the rocking chair she remembered Karen Brody sitting in had been replaced with a newer one. The old one could have broken during the intervening years, but some deep instinct told her that its absence was deliberate.

Deciding that the fact no one was home was the universe telling her she needed some sleep between now and when she faced the Brodys, she headed back to her truck. As she retraced the miles back to Blue Falls, her thoughts narrowed in on falling into bed, into oblivion.

By the time she checked into her room at the Country Vista Inn, she was dead on her feet, barely able to drag her bag into the room. She dropped it just inside the door and headed straight for the bed, not even bothering to change into pajamas.

Despite the fatigue, sleep proved elusive. She tossed and turned, on the verge of tears. All she wanted was a full night of good, solid rest so she could be better equipped to face the Brodys the next day. But as she stared at the ceiling, she remained wide-awake. To make matters worse, her stomach growled like a bear. Well, no wonder. What little she'd consumed that day was lying on the side of the road.

Unable to get comfortable, she sat up on the edge of the bed. Maybe if she got something to eat, the fact that she didn't have to face the

Brodys tonight would allow her to keep a meal down. She continued to sit, letting her mind and stomach adjust to the idea of food. When she didn't feel as if she'd be sick again, she stood, grabbed her purse and went out in search of food.

She drove through downtown Blue Falls, snippets of childhood memories seeming to float in through her open window. Enjoying a cookie at the Mehlerhaus Bakery, watching the annual Christmas parade and tree lighting, sitting by the lake watching the sailboats glide across its shiny surface. As she rolled into the main part of the downtown business district, she saw that the Primrose Café was closed for the evening, as was the bakery. She spotted a Mexican place, but she didn't trust her stomach enough to risk that.

As she continued down Main Street, the sound of music drew her attention. While most of the town seemed to be closed up for the night, the Blue Falls Music Hall was still hopping, if the full parking lot was any indication. The memory was hazy, but she seemed to remember the place having a limited menu from the few times her family had gone on family night, the one night each week when they didn't serve alcohol and thus could admit children. Surely anything they had would beat the vending machine at the motel.

Natalie pulled into one of the few empty parking spots then headed inside. The twangy strands of a country song and the din of conversation hit her as soon as she opened the door. Though she was tired and not particularly in a social mood, losing herself in the crowd held more appeal than staring at the ceiling of her room while the ball of anxiety in the pit of her stomach did its best to consume her.

She weaved a path through the crowd and

finally made her way to the bar. The sight of all the people drinking threatened to cause her nausea to return, but she shook it off. She knew there was nothing wrong with having an occasional drink, but she'd just seen how it could take over and ruin a person's life and damage those around him.

After a deep breath that smelled like equal parts beer, fried food and woodsy aftershave from some nearby cowboy, she crossed the rest of the distance to the bar, arriving just in time to take possession of a bar stool vacated by a woman who'd been asked to dance.

The bartender, a middle-aged guy who wasn't bad-looking, stepped in front of her. "What can I get you?"

She spotted a plate of cheese fries a few seats down from her and realized how long it had been since she'd had one of her favorite guilty pleasures. "I'll take a water and some cheese fries." She just hoped her stomach behaved itself when her own food arrived.

"Coming right up."

Out of all the conversations surrounding her, Natalie's hearing zeroed in on that of two women a couple of stools down from where she sat.

"I can't believe he dumped me," one said, then sniffed.

"He doesn't deserve you," the other replied. "Hey, my friend needs another drink." Obviously, the last was directed at the bartender because he headed that way, dropping off Natalie's water as he passed.

The first woman sounded so brokenhearted, and for a moment Natalie could understand her need to push the real world away with a drink. How much more powerful had the need been for her father considering what he'd done?

She closed her eyes briefly, doing her best to

push away those thoughts or she wouldn't be keeping the fries down long.

"Crowded tonight, isn't it?"

It took Natalie a moment to realize the blond guy in the neatly pressed shirt was talking to her. "Um, yeah."

He glanced back toward the dance floor. "Good song. Would you like to dance?"

She managed a small smile. "Sorry, not tonight."

He grinned back. "Well, at least that leaves the door open for another night."

The guy couldn't know that she wouldn't be in Blue Falls any other night, but she didn't enlighten him, either. Letting him think he had a chance in the future had probably just bought her peace for the one night she was in town.

Or so she thought. By the time her cheese fries arrived, she was beginning to feel like a piece of meat and the only single female in the county. Hoping the heaping plate of fries would keep well-meaning potential dance partners at bay, she took a steadying breath then a bite of a gooey, cheesy fry. As she chewed, she paid close attention to her stomach. But thankfully it seemed to have decided it had done enough damage for the evening.

When the older woman sitting next to Natalie vacated her stool, someone else immediately took her place. Seats at the bar seemed to be a hot commodity.

"You must be new in town," the new bar-stool resident said.

This time Natalie hoped he was talking to her, because he had one of those voices that rumbled from deep within his chest and made a woman go all warm and puddly. Sure, it wouldn't make any difference in how long she planned to stay in town, but she wouldn't mind listening to it while she ate. Maybe he could read the menu to her or something.

"Your fine deductive skills tell you that?" She didn't look at him, afraid that if the face didn't match the voice she'd be unaccountably disappointed.

"Yes. Most people come to the music hall to dance or drink, and you're doing neither."

She tapped her glass. "I'm drinking."

"So you are." There was a hint of a laugh in his voice, and she looked in his direction before thinking.

Whatever she'd been about to say died on her lips because her neighbor's face matched his voice perfectly. Dark eyes looked back at her from a handsome, chiseled face, the kind you'd imagine a romanticized cowboy should have. A hint of dark hair peeked out from under his straw-colored cowboy hat. He wore a white, button-up shirt and what looked like new jeans.

Though she wasn't about to allow herself to continue looking down his body, she had no doubt that he probably also sported a pair of cowboy boots buffed for a night on the town. All in all, he was the epitome of what cowboys called dressed up.

His lips edged up in a grin right before he reached over and nabbed one of her fries. She very nearly smacked his hand, but that was too familiar of a gesture toward someone she didn't know, especially since that someone was currently causing her pulse to stage a footrace through her veins. She wouldn't be the least bit surprised if the bartender pulled out a fire extinguisher to combat the flames that felt as if they were consuming her face.

After a couple of moments, she gave the fry thief a raised-eyebrow look. "You steal food from strangers all the time?"

"Nope. Giving it a trial run."

She couldn't help the laugh that escaped her. This man had no idea how big of a deal it was that he'd drawn a laugh from her. Since the night she'd sat beside her father as he passed from life to death, the sound of a laugh had become as foreign and impossible as traveling to the dark side of the moon.

"I suppose I could share so you're not arrested for food theft." She scooted the large plate to a spot halfway between them. "Lord knows they gave me enough to feed a family of four."

He grabbed another fry. "Don't mind if I do, though I'm friends with the sheriff, so I think I'm safe."

Natalie tried to stay calm and appear unfazed as they munched on a couple of fries. Considering the week she'd had and the reason she was in town, she shouldn't even be able to feel attraction toward a man. And yet she did, one so strong that it had her feeling as if she might suddenly lean toward him and slide off the stool into the floor.

"So what brings you to town?"

She searched for a truth that wasn't the entire truth. "I used to live here when I was a kid."

Before he could respond, the bartender stopped in front of her dinner partner.

"Hey, Garrett. What can I get you to drink?"

Natalie choked on the fry she was in the process of swallowing. She sensed the men staring at her, probably wondering if she needed the Heimlich performed, as she reached for her glass. When she got the cough under control, she took a long drink.

"You okay?" Garrett asked.

Garrett. What were the chances that she'd run into another Garrett who was the right age in a town the size of Blue Falls?

When she noticed him looking at her with concern in those dark eyes, she realized she hadn't responded. "Yeah. Just went down the wrong way."

Natalie's stomach started to turn again, changing the fries from a treat to a disaster waiting to happen. She'd settled into the idea that she wouldn't have to face the Brodys until the next day, and now here she was sitting next to Chloe's older brother. Everything she'd planned to say, the words she'd practiced as the miles ticked by from Wichita, were nothing but a jumbled mess in her head.

Chapter Three

"You sure you're okay?" He sounded so genuinely concerned, and she had to fight the knee-jerk reaction that she didn't deserve it.

She nodded then fiddled with one of the fries but didn't bring it to her mouth. At the moment, she couldn't imagine ever wanting to eat again.

"So, you used to live here, huh?"

Instead of answering, she spun halfway to face him. "Are you Garrett Brody?"

His eyes widened briefly before he tilted his head to the side as if trying to place her. "Do I know you?"

She swallowed and did her best to ignore the

queasiness invading her middle. "Natalie Todd. I used to be friends with Chloe when we were kids."

Garrett tipped his hat back and looked at her closely. His scrutiny made her even more aware of just how good-looking he'd grown up to be, as if carved by a modern-day Michelangelo of cowboys. Not that it surprised her. He'd been cute even as a boy, so much so that he'd been her first crush. Leaving him behind in Blue Falls had broken her heart almost as much as realizing she might never see her best friend again.

"I remember you. The two of you used to be thick as thieves. I also remember Chloe wailing as if the world was ending when you moved away."

Guilt, even though it wasn't her fault, roiled inside her, dancing a tango with her anxiety. "Yeah, it was hard."

Natalie glanced at some of the surrounding patrons, not wanting to go into any more detail in the middle of a room crowded with people who didn't need to hear them. "Are Chloe and Owen here?"

She shifted her attention back to Garrett in time to see him shake his head.

"I just came from Owen's wedding, so he and his new wife are headed to Austin for the night and then the airport in the morning for their honeymoon. Chloe got married recently, too, so all four of them are jetting off to the Caribbean."

God, could fulfilling her father's dying request get any harder? Part of her wanted to just blurt it out to Garrett then race as fast as her truck would take her back to Kansas. But that was the coward's way out, and she wouldn't walk the same road her father had.

While she mentally cursed the entire situation, she grabbed her glass with a hand that was a little too shaky. But Garrett either didn't notice or chose not to comment. She knew she should make her exit and go back to the motel to regroup, but her brain refused to send the appropriate signals to her body to make it move. If she stuck to the plan of telling all of the Brodys at once, she either had to go back home and come back at a later date or stick around until the honeymooners returned. Both options held about as much appeal as lying down on a fire-ant hill covered in honey.

If she went home, she wondered if she'd find the nerve to come back to Blue Falls a second time. But if she stayed, what the hell was she going to do with all the free time? What about her job? And was it fair to Owen and Chloe to hit them with this type of news during what was likely the happiest time of their lives? An ache started throbbing in her forehead between her eyes.

Garrett snatched another French fry, evidently oblivious to her inner turmoil. And she needed to keep it that way.

"They didn't feed you at the wedding reception?"

"Yeah, but there's always room for cheese fries. So, where you living now?"

"Wichita."

"That where you moved when you left Blue Falls?"

Natalie resisted the building urge to flee. "Yeah. You still live at the ranch?"

"Yep, just me and Dad now. Chloe and her husband, Wyatt, have their own place on another part of the property. Owen's living in town, above Linnea's bridal store, but still works out at the ranch."

So, Garrett seemed to be the only unmarried

sibling, and she tried not to be happy about that. His marital status shouldn't matter to her at all. It wasn't as if she had a chance with him, even if hundreds of miles didn't stand between where they lived their lives. Once she revealed why she'd come back to Blue Falls, he would never want to see her again. And she wouldn't be able to blame him.

"What do you do in Wichita?"

"I'm a vet," she said absently, still stuck on why she was sitting here in a town she hadn't seen in two decades.

When Garrett picked up yet another fry, she slid the plate the rest of the way in front of him.

"Sorry. I'll stop stealing your food."

"It's okay. I realized I'm too tired to eat." Another glance at him and the resultant pull she felt toward him was enough to propel her to her feet. "I've had a really long day, so I'm going to call it a night."

As she started to step away, his voice, that delicious voice that could so easily seduce, stopped her.

"How long are you in town? I know Chloe would love to see you and catch up."

The lonely, fragile part of her wanted him to be asking for himself and not Chloe, but she knew her thoughts were irrational. If she managed to get a solid night's sleep, she'd probably wake wondering what had possessed her brain tonight.

"Not sure. But I'll get in touch with her when she returns." She wasn't positive that was true, but she had to put some distance between herself and Garrett before she cracked and spilled everything too soon, in the wrong place. Before he could say anything else, she pushed her way through the crowd toward the door.

By the time she reached the parking lot, she felt genuinely ill, the kind of ill that came from too little food, not enough rest and nerves frazzled almost to the breaking point. As if to match her mood, it started to rain as she drove back to the motel.

This time, she managed to exchange her clothes for her pajamas and slid underneath the covers. She lay on her side, wondering if she'd made the biggest mistake of her life when she'd promised her father that she would deliver his confession and apology. What could possibly be gained from telling the Brodys the truth? All it would do is hurt them by reopening old wounds.

You don't know that.

She hated that voice of doubt in her head, the one that said that maybe the wound was already open, that it had never healed and wouldn't until all their questions had answers, no matter how painful they might be. Plus, she knew herself well enough to realize that if she didn't fulfill her promise to her father, she wouldn't be able to live with herself. Lying was one thing, but lying to a person about to take his last breath was something else entirely. She couldn't let her promise be a lie.

THE NOISE AND activity around Garrett faded as his thoughts zeroed in on the unexpected meet-up with Natalie Todd. He continued to eat the cheese fries she'd left behind and sip on the beer he'd ordered. He had only a vague recollection of what she looked like when she'd been a kid, but she'd certainly grown up to be a beautiful woman. The moment he'd seen her profile as she sat on the bar stool, it'd been as if he'd known he had to sit next to her, talk to her. The totally irrational knowledge that he might have pushed anyone who got in his way out of his path made him pause with a fry half-way to his mouth.

What was going on? Had some sliver of what Chloe said at the reception wormed its way into his brain, putting him in some sort of primal wife-hunting mode? He shook his head and pushed away both the unfinished plate of fries and the three-quarters-full beer bottle.

"Done already?" James Turner, who was tending the bar, gave Garrett a questioning look that also managed to convey that he knew exactly what was going on.

"Yep. Long day."

"Takes a lot of fuss to get two people hitched."

"Amen to that." Garrett pulled out his wallet and placed a five-dollar bill on the bar before standing. He chose to ignore the grin James wasn't even attempting to hide. But as he made his way outside, he found himself wanting to smile, too.

Damn if he didn't feel as he had when he'd been twelve and bumped into Lila Croft as she came out of the girls' locker room after PE. His eyes had locked with hers for a moment before she walked away as if nothing had happened. But he'd fallen head over heels in love in the space of a heartbeat, a great and all-consuming love that had lasted until he'd asked her to a homecoming dance in seventh grade only to be shot down as if he were the ugliest, stinkiest boy on the planet. That had been the end of his foray into instant love.

Lila was married to the owner of a landscaping company in Austin now. He occasionally ran into her and her three kids when she came back to Blue Falls to see her parents, and each time it was as if he'd never harbored any feelings toward her other than a casual acquaintance.

He hurried out into the rain and had just made it to his truck when he heard the unholiest racket. He looked toward the street in time to see the limo filled with his siblings and their spouses rolling through town, all manner of cans tied to the bumper. He laughed and shook his head before hopping into his truck.

He was leaving the city limits before he realized that Natalie hadn't answered his question about why she was in town. As far as he knew, she had no family left here. Thoughts of her accompanied him as he drove toward the ranch, eventually passing out of the rain onto a stretch of road with dry pavement. Her eyes were the kind of bright blue that would make you stare even though you knew it was rude. Her long blond hair had been pulled up into a cute ponytail, but he bet it was gorgeous down and flowing free. And her body…well, he hadn't been the only man in the music hall salivating. It was a miracle she'd made it out of the place without a dozen of them attaching themselves to her like sticky weed.

A flash of lightning in the distance drew his attention a moment before rain started sprinkling on his windshield again. When he pulled into the ranch, he spotted his dad's truck and did his best to put thoughts of Natalie Todd and her perfectly shaped body out of his mind. Last thing he wanted to do was walk into the house aroused.

Thinking of taking a dunk in an icy lake somewhere cold like Minnesota or the far northern reaches of Canada, he stepped out of the truck. The wind kicked up, whistling around the edge of the house like something with a tortured soul. Even Roscoe and Cletus, his family's two basset hounds, were not in their usual spots on the front porch. He imagined they'd toddled off to their doghouse out back.

The thunder and lightning grew closer, but still it only sprinkled. He held on to his hat to keep it from sailing off into the night as he headed for the front steps. When he stepped inside the house, he froze for a moment, the short span of time it took for him to realize that his father was holding one of the family portraits from when Garrett's mom was alive. In the next breath, his dad returned the photo to its spot on the mantel and turned toward him.

"Good night to fly a kite," his dad said, acting as if he hadn't just been having a sentimental moment.

Garrett took off his hat and hung it on the rack by the door. "Maybe if you want to pull a Ben Franklin and get fried."

His dad chuckled and headed for the kitchen. "Glad we got everything squared away before Mother Nature decided to kick up her heels."

As if to reply to that comment, a bright flash outside was quickly followed by a deafening boom of thunder that shook the house. Garrett and his dad both jumped.

"That was close," his dad said.

"Too close." Garrett strode to the window but saw nothing but the darkness beyond the dim glow of the security lamp on the barn.

His dad blew out a breath. "Well, I'm going to turn in. I'm so tired I think I might be able to sleep straight through this racket."

Garrett nodded. After his dad disappeared down the hall, Garrett walked into the kitchen to check out back. A peek through the window didn't show anything amiss, so he, too, headed for bed. Work never ended on a ranch, and that work started early.

He'd just started to unbutton his shirt, his thoughts floating right back to Natalie and the way her lips had moved when she'd smiled, when something made him look out his bedroom window. His heart thumped extra hard when he spotted flames on the roof of the barn.

Thankful he was still wearing his boots, he

ran out into the hall. "Dad, call the fire department! The barn's on fire!"

His dad stuck his head out of his bedroom door. "What?"

"Lightning hit the barn."

He raced to the barn, hoping the sprinkles would vacate in favor of a downpour to put out the blaze. Already, the horses were agitated, whinnying and unable to stand still in their stalls. Another loud clap of thunder caused Bronson, his dad's horse, to kick at his stall as his eyes went wide with fear.

Garrett hurried to get the horses out of the barn without causing injury to them or himself, not an easy task. He didn't like taking them out into the storm, but it was better than a burning roof caving in on them if the fire department didn't arrive in time to extinguish the flames.

By the time he got to the stall holding Penelope, Chloe's horse was about to lose her mind with fear. The fire was centered right above the bay mare's head, so he could understand. But as he tried to calm her, she was having none of it. As he started to ease the stall door open, Penelope kicked, busting a couple of the slats with her powerful hooves.

"Come on, girl, let's get out of here."

But the horse still didn't cooperate, and Garrett was afraid the next thing she kicked would be him. He took a side step just in time as she panicked and busted out of the stall. The horse screamed as she broke free and raced out of the barn. Garrett fell back into the dirt, rolling to avoid being trampled.

The fire trucks coming up the driveway halted Penelope's flight in that direction. She changed course, only to find herself cornered against the corral fence on one side, Garrett's dad on another and finally Garrett as he stumbled out of the barn.

Penelope spun, panic driving her movements, her need to flee. Garrett's heart nearly stopped when he saw a large sliver of wood protruding from the horse's side. They had to calm her down and get the vet out here, while making sure the barn didn't burn down and the other horses didn't break from where he and his dad had tied them several yards down the fence line.

Out of the corner of his eye, Garrett saw the firefighters hopping out of the trucks and retrieving hoses and gear. But even if the barn burned down to a pile of ash, he had to keep his attention on Penelope. He hated to see an animal in pain, and he couldn't let her injure herself further. He couldn't stand the idea of his sister coming home from her belated honeymoon to find her horse severely injured or worse.

"Easy, girl," he said, trying to sound soothing even though his heart was doing its best to beat out of his chest. He slowly moved closer to Penelope, continuing to talk to the frightened animal.

It took what felt like forever to get Penelope calmed down enough that Garrett figured she wouldn't injure herself further. But if the thunder kept up or the fire grew any bigger, he wasn't betting she wouldn't break free again and run until she collapsed or bled to death.

His dad didn't have to be told to go call Dr. Franklin. He just headed for the house once he saw Garrett had Penelope under control.

With another roll of thunder, the heavens finally turned on the spigot and rain started falling harder. It took less than a minute for Garrett's clothes to be soaked through, but he didn't move.

His dad stalked back across the yard. "Doc Franklin is out of town, so I put a call in to Dr.

Smith over in Fredericksburg. But his answering service said he's out on another call. We're next up."

The way Penelope was bleeding and breathing hard, they needed help sooner. He glanced back over his shoulder but didn't see flames anymore. Thank God for that. He returned his attention to his dad.

"Watch her. I've got an idea."

He raced into the house and grabbed the phone. Since he'd been at the Wildflower Inn earlier and didn't think Natalie was staying there, he called the next best guess for where she was staying.

"Country Vista Inn," a female voice answered.

"Natalie Todd's room, please."

When the person on the other end of the line didn't come back with a "There's no one staying here by that name," instead connecting him with a room, he almost breathed a sigh of relief. But when the phone rang several times with no answer, he started pacing and ran his fingers through his hair.

"Come on, pick up."

As if she heard him, Natalie's sleepy voice said, "Hello?"

Despite all the potential catastrophes currently in play, for a moment he stood there imagining her in bed, that blond hair rumpled, her feminine curves clothed in something soft and barely there.

Good grief, he needed to get laid.

"Natalie, it's Garrett Brody. Sorry to wake you, but I need your help."

She didn't immediately respond, and for a moment he wondered if she'd fallen back asleep.

"My help?"

"You're a vet, and I have a badly injured horse."

"Doesn't Blue Falls have a vet?"

"Dr. Franklin is out of town, and the backup from Fredericksburg is already on another call. And Chloe's horse has a big piece of wood piercing her side."

He heard movement on the other end of the call and imagined her swinging her legs over the edge of the bed.

"Please tell me you're like Dr. Franklin and pack medical supplies with you wherever you go," he said.

"I do," Natalie said through a yawn. "I'll be there in a few minutes."

Thank goodness for small miracles. He headed back outside to tell his dad the news, determined not to imagine Natalie arriving in her skimpy sleepwear and bed-tousled hair. Damn if he didn't get a raging hard-on at that image. This time, he was thankful to be doused by the cold rain.

Chapter Four

Natalie exchanged her pajamas for jeans and a T-shirt. The absolute last thing she wanted to do was go back out to the Brody ranch again and still not be able to tell them why she was in town. Well, she could tell Garrett and his dad, but it just didn't feel right to not tell Chloe. After all, they'd once been very close. To give the information to the first Brody she could find then race back to Kansas before Chloe even returned from her honeymoon felt like the ultimate in cowardice. If she was going to do this, she was going to do it right, no matter how hard it proved to be.

But now, she had to focus on the task at hand. She might not want to be around the Brodys until she could talk to all of them at once, but she couldn't leave an animal in danger.

The rain was still coming down as she raced out to her truck and drove as fast as she dared toward the Brodys' ranch. Her stomach knotted, and she hoped the few fries she'd eaten stayed right where they were.

The drive seemed to take three times as long as it had earlier, even counting the stop she'd had to make on the side of the road during the first trip. The rain didn't slacken until she neared the turn into the ranch, and then only slightly. She hit the brakes, skidding a little, when she came over a small hill and saw two fire trucks pulling out of the Brodys' drive.

Her heart lurched. Fire trucks? She glanced across the darkened field and made out a lighted window through the slanting rain. At least something was still standing. And Garrett had said nothing about a fire when he'd called. She didn't think something could have caught fire, the 911 call be made, fire trucks respond and the fire be extinguished in the half hour it had taken her to arrive.

When the trucks passed her, she pulled into the drive and hurried to reach the house. Her headlights caught someone leading two horses toward the barn. The man looked over his shoulder toward her, and though she couldn't tell for certain, she got the feeling it was Garrett's dad.

A huge lump formed in her throat and she had to blink back tears. Her father had cost Mr. Brody his wife, the mother of his children. How in the world was she going to face him and not have the horrible truth be obvious in her expression?

Now is not the time. Now you focus on work, a hurt animal, nothing else.

Not even the tall, sexy and currently drenched man she saw beyond the one leading the horses. Even soaking wet and with her vision impaired by the rain battling with her windshield wipers, she knew it was Garrett standing next to a big bay, his hand slowly rubbing down the horse's neck.

She shook her head as she parked then grabbed the emergency medical kit she kept with her at all times. She never knew when she might come upon an animal in need, whether it was livestock, pet or wildlife. She cared for all of their welfare equally.

Not taking time to retrieve her rain gear, she hopped out of the truck and crossed to where Garrett stood next to the beautiful animal.

"I didn't know whether to move her," he said

without preamble. He nodded toward the barn. "We had a fire, but it's out now."

She stepped close to the mare, shushing her when she tried to sidestep away. Running her hand along the same stretch of neck that Garrett had moments earlier, she said, "There's a good girl." She examined the injury as best she could in the dim light. "Bring her inside, but carefully. Try not to let her move any more than she has to."

Natalie led the way inside the barn, which smelled like a combination of hay, rain and smoke. She glanced up to where the back part of the building's roof now sported a hole that would make the last two stalls unusable until repairs were made. Of course, one of those stalls also had damage of its own that had nothing to do with the roof damage. She had no doubt that the injured horse had been the one to splinter the wood on the front of the stall.

She pointed toward the smallest stall near the front of the barn. "Put her in there."

"Won't give you much room to work."

"Also won't give her room to kick me into next week."

Natalie stayed clear until Garrett managed to get the animal into the stall. He did his best to soothe the mare, but she still didn't go into the stall willingly.

"Be careful," he said when Natalie stepped into the stall. "I don't want you getting hurt."

She eased her hand along the horse's side, gradually moving toward the spot where the sizable sliver of wood was protruding. "Try to keep her as calm as you can. Keep talking to her, draw her attention that direction."

Natalie went into a familiar autopilot mode, opening her bag of veterinary supplies and prepping everything she'd need. When she was ready to remove the mother of all splinters, she caught Garrett's eye across the mare's back. "Get ready. I'm going to pull out our offender."

Thankfully, the wood hadn't gone too deep into the horse's flesh, but that didn't make much difference to the mare's reaction when Natalie jerked it out. The animal threw her head back, showing her teeth, and sidestepped so suddenly that she slammed Natalie against the side of the stall.

"You okay?" Garrett sounded so concerned that the lump made a return appearance in her throat.

"Yeah, I'm good." Deliberately not making eye contact with him, she went to work cleaning the wound, disinfecting and closing it up. "What's this girl's name anyway?"

"Penelope."

"Interesting name for a horse."

"Chloe named it after a character in one of her favorite movies."

Before she could stop herself, she glanced toward Garrett and found him watching her. Even looking as if he'd been dumped in the lake, he still took her breath away. For a moment she forgot what she'd been about to say. It took forcing herself to break eye contact to get her brain functioning again. "The movie *Penelope*?"

"Yeah. She's probably seen that movie a hundred times."

"It's a good one." In fact, it was one of Natalie's favorites, too. But instead of making her happy that she and her childhood friend still obviously had things in common, a heavy sadness welled up in her. She'd missed so much of Chloe's life, so many adventures they might have had together if her father had simply not gotten in his car that night.

She shoved away that thought because she needed to concentrate on her task. When she finally finished, she caressed the side of

Penelope's face and scratched between her ears. "Good girl. You've had a rough night, huh?"

Seemingly calmer than she'd been since Natalie arrived, Penelope turned her head and nuzzled Natalie's face.

"Well, wonders never cease."

Natalie glanced toward the stall's door and saw Garrett's dad standing there with his forearms propped along the top of the door. Her heart ached in her chest. He looked so much older than she remembered. Even though that made perfect sense, the realization also made her sad.

When he looked at her and smiled, she had to fight tears.

"When Garrett told me you were in town and you were a vet, I couldn't believe it." He shook his head slowly. "You're not that little girl I remember."

She made herself smile back. "Not for a long time."

"Lot's changed since those days." He nodded toward Penelope. "Looks like you could give Dr. Franklin a run for his money."

"So he's really still the vet here?"

"Yep."

As she packed up her supplies, she couldn't help a small smile, a real one this time. She had fond memories of Dr. Franklin, of helping out around his vet practice when her mom had volunteered there one day a week. Those hours spent watching him take care of sick animals had been what set her on the path to becoming a veterinarian herself.

She put the brakes on the trip down memory lane and slipped out of the stall, Garrett right behind her.

"After this night, we all need a big slice of pie," Garrett's dad said.

"That's okay. I'll just be going." She needed to get away from the ranch, from the memories, from the way her pulse sped up every time she made eye contact with Garrett. Hell, every time she was within sight of him. It wasn't helping that with his clothes plastered to his skin, she could see every well-defined muscle and wanted to skim her hands over them.

Mr. Brody patted her on the shoulder. "I insist. Someone has to save me from Linnea's baking."

She glanced at Garrett.

"Owen's new wife," he said. "She really likes to bake when she's nervous."

"And these last few days leading up to the wedding, she's been going through sugar like we operate a sugar cane plantation instead of a cattle ranch." Mr. Brody chuckled. "Not that I'm complaining." He patted his middle. "But the girl is going to make me fat."

Natalie couldn't help smiling. She'd always loved Mr. Brody. Though she would always feel guilty afterward, she'd sometimes imagined what life would have been like if he were her dad instead of her own.

"You still look young and trim to me," she said.

"Oh, I like you." Mr. Brody put his arm around her. "Let's get this angel of mercy some pie."

Natalie's heart ached at the way Mr. Brody had described her. She couldn't help thinking how he might hate her when she revealed why she'd come back to Blue Falls and how that would break her heart. Everything inside her screamed to dig in her heels, to not allow Garrett and his dad to usher her inside. The thought of her father's letter sitting in her luggage at the motel burned as if it were taped right over her heart.

But if she protested too much, that would send up red flags she wasn't ready to explain. She cursed the incredibly bad timing of her arrival as she followed Mr. Brody through the slackened rain and up the front steps she'd climbed earlier when no one was home.

She toed off her muddy boots on the porch. When she stepped through the front door, she nearly gasped at how the past came careening at her and slammed into her chest. Everything looked the same, exactly as she remembered it. The couch and chairs, the same beige and dark brown leather set, still sat configured the way they had been when she was a child. Framed photos still covered every inch of the mantel above the fireplace that got used only during the dead of winter. She half expected Karen Brody to come walking out of the kitchen, wiping her hands on a towel and announcing there were cookies fresh from the oven.

"You okay?"

She tore her gaze away from the time capsule that was the Brody living room to look up at Garrett. Though he was probably every bit as chilled as she was, she'd swear she could feel heat coming off his body.

"Uh, yeah. Just tired, I guess."

The edge of his mouth edged up in a grin. "I know the feeling." He nodded toward the kitchen. "Come on. Lin's pie is really good."

"Want some coffee?" his dad asked when they entered the kitchen.

She shook her head. "No. I need to get some sleep when I go back to the motel."

When Garrett pulled out a chair for her, her heart rate sped up. With a slight smile, she sat. "Thanks."

She watched as Mr. Brody sliced three large pieces of chocolate meringue pie and placed them on small plates. When he slid hers in front of her, her stomach growled audibly.

"Just in time, by the sound of it," he said.

Garrett took the chair next to her. "You didn't eat enough of your fries earlier."

"I guess not."

She mentally crossed her fingers that the pie wouldn't upset her stomach, especially when she took the first bite. "This is delicious."

So good, in fact, that she quickly took a couple more bites.

"Hard to believe you're sitting here in our kitchen again," Mr. Brody said, knocking her off her pie high. "Garrett says you live in Kansas. How are your parents doing?"

The question brought back a flood of unwelcome memories from the past week, and she slowly placed her fork on the plate beside her half-eaten slice of pie. She tried to swallow past that persistent lump in her throat but found it impossible.

"Mom's okay, but my dad…" Her voice broke as she stared at the top of the meringue. "He passed away recently." She purposely didn't share how recently, wanting to avoid questions about why she was in Texas so soon after her father's death.

"I'm sorry to hear that."

Panic shot to life in her middle and quickly invaded the rest of her body. *Please don't ask me why I'm here.*

An awkward silence hung in the air for a moment before Mr. Brody spoke again. "Are your sisters in Kansas, too? They were just little-bitty things when you moved away."

She tried swallowing again and was a little more successful this time. "Allison is. She lives in Kansas City with her family and is an elementary school teacher. But Renee actually lives in Paris, France. She's an artist. You'd never know she's a Midwestern girl if you saw her now."

"Do you get to see her much?" Garrett asked.

She shifted her gaze to him and was momentarily entranced by how good he looked despite the fact he'd been doused by rain and had a dirty streak across his cheek. Or maybe he looked good because of it. "Um, she flies home about once a year. Of course, she was home for…"

When he nodded in understanding, she didn't have to finish the sentence.

For a moment, she considered telling them the truth, but it just felt bone-deep wrong. They seemed happy. And despite the fact that only Mr. Brody and Garrett sat at the table with her, she felt the familiar love that resided in this house. Part of her yearned to embrace it, to bask in that wonderful feeling. Her family loved each other, but that love had always existed alongside the strain of having an alcoholic for a father. She knew that in the larger scheme of things she'd been lucky. Her dad hadn't been a mean drunk. He never would have dreamed of hurting his wife and daughters.

But he'd killed a woman, a kindhearted, loving wife and mother who'd been ripped from the men now seated with Natalie. A sudden ache of wrongness filled her middle, a feeling that she had no right to sit here and eat pie with them, acting as if everything was okay.

Natalie scooted her chair away from the table. "Thanks for the pie, but I need to be going."

"Okay. Sorry to have pulled you out here in the middle of the night," Mr. Brody said.

"No, it's okay. I'm glad I could help."

She stood and glanced at Garrett only for a moment, enough to see he was getting to his feet. She had to get out of the house before it finished closing in on her. "Good night."

She didn't run, but she ate up the ground between her and the front door so quickly that she was halfway down the steps before Garrett reached the porch behind her.

"Natalie?"

Why couldn't he just let her go? But if she ignored him and ran, she might break down and spill everything when she was only hanging on by a thread, when she would do it all wrong.

Garrett came to stand beside her on the steps, but she didn't look at him.

"I'm sorry if talking about your dad upset you."

"It's okay. I'm just really exhausted and need to get some sleep."

"Are you sure you're okay to drive back into town? We've got plenty of empty bedrooms now."

God, no, that was the last thing she needed to

do, spend the entire night under the same roof as Garrett and his father.

"I'll be fine. Just call Dr. Franklin when he gets back and have him check on Penelope." Before he could say anything else or she could break, she hurried through the drizzle to her truck and got off the Brody ranch as fast as she could without it looking like exactly what it was—fleeing.

GARRETT STOOD ON the front steps watching as Natalie's taillights disappeared into the night. It was the second time she'd run away from him in one evening. No wonder he wasn't in a serious relationship if he made women run off into the night. That sure was great for a guy's ego.

Something tugged on his brain, an instinct demanding to be acknowledged though he couldn't pinpoint what it was trying to say. Hell, maybe he was just bone tired like Natalie.

As he dragged himself back into the house, his dad was coming out of the kitchen. "I hope I didn't run her off."

"I think we're all just ready to call it a day."

"Yeah, my bed is screaming my name."

After his dad wandered off down the hallway, Garrett returned to his own room. But even as wiped out as he was, he couldn't go to sleep. He kept replaying every moment he'd spent with Natalie since bumping into her at the music hall earlier. As soon as he'd seen her, his entire body had started buzzing as if it'd been inhabited by a colony of bees. He hadn't experienced that sort of reaction to a woman in…well, ever. And quite honestly it freaked him out.

He wasn't a complicated guy. Pretty much what he wanted out of life was to carry on the Brody tradition of operating and improving the ranch and have a family of his own. While Owen had been the playboy of the family, dating so many girls that Garrett could never keep them straight, that kind of life had never appealed to Garrett. Some might see that as boring, but he didn't think so. He chose to view it as responsible and not trying to be something he wasn't. He might not be a bad boy, but he had to believe that somewhere out there a wonderful woman was looking for a good guy who would treat her right, a woman who would share his love of the land and a simple, satisfying life. But so far, that woman hadn't crossed his path.

Or had she?

He didn't know Natalie Todd anymore, hadn't really known her when they'd been kids. She'd been Chloe's sidekick, a little blonde girl who'd seemed to love spending time at his house. The adult version didn't have that same bright openness he remembered. But a lot could happen to a person in twenty years, things that changed them. He knew that from bitter experience.

And something was definitely bothering her. Whether it was fatigue as she claimed, the fact that her father had died recently or something else entirely, he had no idea. But both times she'd walked away from him, he'd wanted to bring her back so he could get to know her better. Which made very little sense when he thought about it.

Even though he still didn't know why she was in Blue Falls, he doubted it was because she was planning to move back. So the fact that they lived hours apart, with the entire state of Oklahoma and half the height of Texas separating them, made even thinking about pursuing her all kinds of stupid. He wasn't the kind of guy who was able to sleep with a woman one night and walk away from her the next day as if it was no big deal.

Garrett rolled onto his side and watched as rivulets of rain rolled down his window. He hoped that Natalie had gotten back to the motel okay. Part of him wanted to reach for the phone to call her, to make sure, but she was most likely back in bed, and he didn't want to bother her again tonight.

Even if he liked the idea of hearing her voice as he lay there in the dark.

He ran his hand down over his face. With a new hole in the barn roof as well as a week ahead of being a man down on the ranch, the last thing he had time for was daydreaming about a woman who wasn't even in the realm of possibility for him. And yet that's exactly where Natalie stayed as he replayed the sight of her taking charge with Penelope and calming the animal as she worked on the mare's injury. Those few minutes of watching her work were all he needed to know that she was good at her job, that she was used to working with large animals and cared about their welfare every bit as much as he did. She was no doubt intimately familiar with ranching operations, with his way of life. Not to mention she was stunningly beautiful.

Damn, he wished she still lived in Blue Falls. If she did, he had no doubt he'd pursue her. But as usual, one of the pieces just didn't line up. Story of his life.

But even if that was a dead-end road, it didn't mean he couldn't indulge in a little fantasizing as he drifted toward sleep. Maybe he'd wake up to find that out-of-sync piece had slipped into place sometime in the night.

Chapter Five

Natalie spent almost all of Sunday catching up on the sleep she had missed during the past week. What little time she was awake, she spent microwaving and eating the couple of frozen dinners she'd picked up at the convenience store on the edge of town. She tried watching TV and going for a short walk, but the fatigue continued to weigh her down as if she hadn't slept a wink.

She still felt as if she could sleep another twenty-four hours straight when she awoke midmorning on Monday, but her growling stomach had other ideas. Her miserable eating habits of the past several days had finally caught up to her, trumping any anxiety that made eating difficult. Feeling as if her stomach was caving in and wanting a real meal, she dragged herself from bed and to the shower. The stream of water woke her enough that she didn't look too much like a zombie extra on *The Walking Dead* when she exited her room.

A beautiful day greeted her, one of those fresh and clean days that came after a rain when the sky was wide, blue and for a brief moment free of so much cut-it-with-a-knife humidity and haze. She knew it wouldn't last long, this being Central Texas, so she decided to take full advantage and walked toward the downtown area instead of driving. It was only a handful of blocks to the Primrose Café anyway.

She sank into a chair at a table near the front window and looked at the menu. She'd arrived just in time to hit the end of the breakfast time slot, so she ordered French toast and bacon when the waitress came by.

It wasn't surprising that her entry had drawn a few curious looks. Even with Blue Falls being a tourist destination for wildflower enthusiasts and day-trippers wanting to poke around its variety of shops, every unfamiliar face was likely met with curiosity and speculation. And though she'd once been a local, it was so long ago that she might as well have walked into town for the first time an hour ago.

Hoping to appear casual and unaffected, she grabbed a newspaper off the vacant table next to her and flipped it open. She skimmed the local news, surprised to recognize the occasional name. It shouldn't be shocking that people she'd gone to school with were still around, but for some reason it was. As if when she'd left Blue Falls behind, everything she remembered about it had been altered or deleted entirely.

She startled when someone plopped down into the chair opposite her. When she looked over the top of the paper, she saw a face that she would recognize anywhere. For the first time in what felt like ages, she really and truly smiled. Dr. Harry Franklin grinned back at her the same way he had when she'd been a kid. Though the lines on his face were deeper and more plentiful, she still expected him to reach into his pocket for a sour-apple candy for her.

"You haven't changed a bit," she said.

"You, my dear, are a liar. But I'm glad to see you anyway."

Natalie folded the paper and tossed it on the empty chair beside her.

"I hear I owe you a huge thanks for helping out at the Brody ranch Saturday night," he said.

"It was nothing."

Dr. Franklin was right, she was a liar. The time she'd spent at the ranch had stirred up a confusing mixture of nervousness, curiosity, guilt and yearning inside her. When she'd fled into the night, she'd been convinced it was guilt that had been the impetus. She'd been halfway back to the motel before she realized the yearning had been equally responsible. A yearning for closeness, happiness and, yes, Garrett Brody. She forced that thought to the back of her brain, hoping it would disappear into the file of forgotten things, wherever those resided.

"That also is not true. You did a good thing, and I appreciate it. And may I just say that it makes my heart happy that you became a veterinarian. You were always so good with the animals, especially the ones that really needed a little extra TLC. They could sense that about you, your kind heart."

Dr. Franklin's words made tears pool in her eyes. She blinked a few times to keep from making a fool of herself. She could see the headline now—Local Vet Makes Woman Cry in Primrose Café.

He reached across the table and patted her hand. "Aw, now, sweetie, I didn't mean to make you all misty-eyed."

She smiled. "I'm okay. It just means a lot to hear you say that. Those days I spent at your clinic with Mom, that's what made me want to become a vet."

"No surprise there. You're a natural. Your mama used to have to almost drag you out of the clinic. I think you would have slept there if she'd let you."

She certainly would have. That would have been more peaceful than worrying about her drunken father coming home late and tripping over the furniture, waking up her sisters. Natalie couldn't remember a time when she hadn't felt protective of Allison and Renee, when she hadn't felt more adult than child.

Well, that wasn't true. Those wonderful times spent at the Brody ranch, where Chloe's parents had treated her like the child she was, had been her sole reprieve. She treasured those memories of playing with new kittens in the barn, splashing in the creek that only came up to their ankles after a rain, board games and fresh-baked cookies. She'd been able to relax at Chloe's house, something that was much rarer at her own.

There had been so many nights when she'd lain in bed at home listening to her father's slurred speech and his inability to walk straight making him bounce into chairs and tables like one of those metal balls in a pinball machine. She'd had to grip her sheet in her hands to tether herself to the bed so she wouldn't climb out the window and walk all the way to the Brody ranch.

The waitress brought Dr. Franklin a steaming cup of coffee and a plain glazed doughnut. He smiled up at the young woman. "Thanks, Daisy."

Daisy smiled back before heading over to check on a table of older ladies.

"So, what brings you back to town?"

The question shouldn't have caught Natalie off guard, but it did. She really should have had an answer ready to go before she arrived in Blue Falls, but somehow that necessity hadn't made its way through all the other thoughts bombarding her brain.

"Just had a few days off and thought I'd take a road trip."

"Well, I'm glad you did. I've thought of you often through the years."

Please don't ask me why we left.

Thankfully, he didn't.

"Same here," she said. "Especially when I

was in vet school and wondering if I'd make it through."

"How's your family?"

"Okay." She didn't feel up to explaining about her dad being gone, where her sisters were and what they were doing.

Dr. Franklin nodded once, as if her single-word answer was enough for him.

"What about yours?" she asked.

"Oh, Sheila is still putting up with me. We just went to the coast to visit Tim and spoil the grandkids. We were taking a walk on the beach when you saved the day."

"Do you get to see them often?"

"Not as much as I'd like, but I hope to retire one of these days and relocate closer to them."

Natalie experienced a pang even though she wouldn't be around to see it. "I can't imagine Blue Falls without you here."

"We all leave at some point, willingly or not."

She thought he was probably talking about death forcing a person to leave, but she wasn't sure there wasn't more to his words. When his gaze met hers, she wondered if Dr. Franklin was as intuitive about people as he was his four-legged patients. Fear squeezed her heart. He couldn't possibly know what her father had done, could he?

But the way he took a large bite of his doughnut in the next moment made her think she was simply being paranoid.

"Have you seen the Brodys' horse since you got back?" she asked, then realized that she probably shouldn't have brought up anything to do with the Brodys. But it was too late now.

"Actually, I'm going to let you do that since I hear you took such good care of the mare the other night."

She shook her head. "I can't."

"It shouldn't take long, and you did the initial care. Plus, I've got appointments stacked up to my eyeballs today. That's the problem with taking days off."

Natalie searched for some way to get out of having to go to the Brody ranch yet again. Even after several hours of sleep, she didn't feel anywhere near ready to face them again, to see Garrett and perhaps become even more attracted to a man who could never be a part of her life, not after she revealed her true purpose for being in Blue Falls.

"Plus, I'm slowing down," Dr. Franklin continued. "I'm just not as quick and spry as I used to be. You'd be doing me a huge favor."

How could she possibly refuse the man who'd been so kind to her when she'd really needed it, the man who had introduced her to her life's passion? The man who had once given her a puppy to be "her special friend." Now that she was an adult, she realized that he had probably seen how hard life had been for her and that she'd needed that puppy every bit as much as it had needed her.

She couldn't refuse such a simple request, but how did she manage to keep getting in these situations where she couldn't say no?

So she found herself nodding, agreeing to walk right back onto that ranch with her awful secret still festering inside her. On her stroll to the Primrose, she'd even been considering driving back to Kansas today, returning to Blue Falls later, when all the Brodys were in residence and the newlyweds had enjoyed a few weeks of married bliss before she became the harbinger of heartbreaking news.

Dr. Franklin rapped his knuckles on the table. "Great! You are a lifesaver." He stood. "And when you're done out at the ranch, come by the clinic. I'd love to hear more about your life now, and I could use an extra set of capable hands."

It was on her lips to say she'd be willing to take on his entire patient load at the clinic if he'd just go to the ranch to do the follow-up visit with Penelope. But that had red flags and too many potential questions written all over it, so she sucked it up and said she'd pop by the clinic after she was finished with Penelope.

Her stomach threatened to twist into knots again, but damn it, she fully intended to enjoy an actual meal. She couldn't keep functioning on a bite here and a nibble there. If she had to go to the ranch again, she needed her body and especially her mind operating at a much higher level than they had been during her previous visit.

Partly because she needed the time to mentally prepare herself for facing the Brodys again but mainly because she frankly was starving, she allowed herself to eat at a leisurely pace as she perused the rest of the *Blue Falls Gazette*.

She even laughed a little when she saw a picture of Greg Bozeman standing out in front of the garage his dad had owned when they were kids. He had the same mischievous grin on his face that she remembered from a day in first grade when he'd put a toad in Mrs. Shackleton's desk, causing her to scream as if she'd opened the door to Freddy Krueger.

After eating the last bite of her French toast and wiping her mouth, she took a deep breath. She couldn't put off checking up on Penelope any longer. So she left enough money on the table for her bill and a tip and walked back to the motel to retrieve her truck.

The drive out to the ranch was peaceful, if you didn't count the ball of twitching nerves currently occupying her middle. When she pulled up the driveway and parked, she spotted Mr. Brody staring up at the top of the barn, where it appeared roofers were at work fixing the hole caused by the fire.

"Hey there," he said when he spotted her. "Doc Franklin said you'd be coming out today. Must say, you're a good bit prettier than he is."

For the second time that day, an old friend made her smile. If felt so good after the past several days, as if the ability to smile was lifting some of the weight off her heart. She glanced around the main part of the ranch, searching for Garrett. But he was nowhere to be seen. She told herself that was a good thing, that she needed to forget how her brain seemed determined to fixate on him and the way her body went on high alert when he was near.

"Garrett's out riding the fence line today, making sure the storm didn't do any damage. Don't want our herd wandering out into any roads."

Natalie turned to retrieve her bag of vet supplies from her truck so that Mr. Brody wouldn't see the blush rushing into her cheeks. Had she really been that obvious about scanning their surroundings for a glimpse of Garrett? But how could she not? Despite everything she was hiding and the number of years she'd been away, Garrett Brody still made her heart race. But while she'd liked him as a kid, that had been puppy love, the first brush with liking a boy. This attraction now, it was entirely different.

His strong, lanky frame, sexy voice and handsome face were enough to make any woman's knees go weak, a perfect male specimen in her book. Too bad he wasn't a complete stranger she'd met in Kansas, where maybe something could come from the wild and instant attraction she'd felt toward him two nights before when he'd stolen that first cheese fry.

Though she really liked Mr. Brody, she hoped he would stay outside the barn. But that wasn't to be. He accompanied her and she searched for something, anything to say that had nothing to do with Garrett or the real reason she was in Blue Falls.

"So, tell me about Chloe's husband," she said as she entered the stall where Penelope stood.

"Wyatt's a good guy, a former bull rider. She patched him up after he got gored, and that was that. My little girl fell in love. What about you? Married? Got a guy back home?"

Well, so much for steering to safer subjects.

"Nope, too busy."

"Nobody's too busy for love. Life isn't meant to be lived alone." The sadness in his voice made her heart ache. "I'm glad Chloe and Owen have found good people to love. Now if I can get Garrett settled, I'll die a happy man."

She gasped and felt her eyes widen as she looked at him.

He waved off her concern. "Don't worry. I'm

still as healthy as a man my age can be. But it's just something you think about when you have children. You'll see someday."

The idea of having children seemed so unattainable, what with not having anyone special in her life with whom to make those children. Part of her had started to think of her dog and two cats as her children, that they were the closest she'd ever have to kids of her own. As she stood there examining Penelope's wound, glad to see there were no signs of infection, she wondered when she'd stopped thinking she'd marry and have children and instead started focusing all her energy on work. When anyone needed a shift covered, she was always the first one to volunteer. Had she worked so much to fill a hole in her life she didn't consciously realize was there?

"You okay?"

She glanced at Mr. Brody. "Yes, why?"

"You looked as if you'd drifted off some-where far away."

"No, just thinking that Penelope here was a lucky girl. Her injury could have been much worse."

Mr. Brody didn't look as if he believed her, but she ignored his doubt.

"So, she's doing well, then?" he finally asked.

She nodded. "Keep an eye on the wound. As long as there are no signs of infection, she should be good as new before you know it." She let Penelope nuzzle her hand before she gathered her supplies and exited the stall.

"Have you had lunch?"

"I ate a late breakfast, so I'm good." She headed out of the barn, intent on leaving before Garrett returned and scattered her brain cells like a gust of wind hitting the puffy head of a dandelion.

When she caught a momentary look of disappointment in Mr. Brody's eyes, the guilt almost choked her. She could tell him the truth right now, right here, and she'd never have to face the rest of the Brody clan. Instead of seeing anger and pain in an entire family's eyes, she'd have to contend with only one set. But she couldn't make the words form, probably because her heart knew it wasn't right. They would need each other to lean on, and she needed it all done in one fell swoop because she feared she'd break down, too.

Even if that meant she had to face Garrett and the hyperaware effect he had on her.

"Plus, I promised Dr. Franklin I'd come by the clinic and lend him a hand." She forced a smile, hating that in the days ahead she would hurt this dear man.

"I'm sure he'll be thankful for the help. But it's a standing invitation. You come out and see us anytime, okay?"

She nodded because she was afraid of what her voice might reveal. Before she lost her tenuous grip on her emotions, she hurried from the barn. The way her luck was going, she half expected to slam right into Garrett. But he was still absent as she crossed to her truck and drove away from the ranch with her horrible secret yet again.

A couple of miles up the road, she spotted someone on a horse in the distance. She slowed then pulled off to the side of the road. Even though he was too far away to see his face, she knew it was Garrett. Though she hadn't seen him atop a horse since she was a young girl, there was no denying how natural he looked, as if he and the animal were one.

There were people who had no need to go out into the world and find themselves because they were perfect right where they were. Garrett Brody was one of those people, just like his father before him. There was something deep and very attractive about that to her. Though she'd lived in Kansas for more than twenty years, it didn't feel like home. She'd never understood why she felt that way considering she'd left Blue Falls so long ago. The town was nearly as foreign to her as Alaska or Austria.

As she watched Garrett ride along the fence line, she envied his absolute rightness here in this place. Though she had a family, a home and a job she enjoyed, an overwhelming sense of being alone and adrift washed over her.

Before Garrett spotted her or rode any closer, she pulled back onto the road and headed toward town. That image of Garrett, the romantic ideal of a cowboy riding the range, refused to vacate her thoughts as she pulled up in front of Dr. Franklin's clinic and walked inside.

"Just in time," Dr. Franklin called out as soon as she stepped into the waiting area. "Dr. Natalie Todd, this is Kylie Forbes. And this hand-some fella," he said as he pointed toward an enormous, tawny-colored Neapolitan mastiff, "is Peanut."

She nearly laughed at the diminutive name for the dog.

"I figured out of all my waiting patients, he's the closest to what you're used to."

That he was, more similar in size to the horses and cattle she regularly saw than the tiny York-shire terrier sitting on the lap of another woman in the corner.

Natalie leaned down eye to eye with the dog. "Hello, Peanut. What seems to be the trouble today?"

Kylie rubbed Peanut's head. "He's got a lump in one of his legs."

Dr. Franklin directed Natalie toward an exam room, and Kylie followed with her canine com-panion. A few minutes later, as Natalie moved next to the examination table where Peanut was lying, the dog raised his head and licked her cheek.

"Peanut, no!" Kylie looked at Natalie. "I'm so sorry."

Natalie just laughed, her heart lifting more than it had in days. "It's okay. I'll take doggie kisses all day long." She petted Peanut's massive head. "Now let's check out your boo-boo."

She ended up removing a lump from Peanut's leg with assurances that Dr. Franklin would let Kylie know the results of the tests as soon as he could. Next up was a cat that had gotten into a fight with a bigger badass kitty followed by a beagle that hadn't been eating. A parade of small animals with various ailments filled her afternoon, keeping Natalie so busy that it was quitting time before she realized it.

When she finished with her last patient, a pet rabbit that had been feeling under the weather, she wandered into Dr. Franklin's office and plopped down into the chair next to the same scarred wooden desk he'd used when she was a kid.

"You need to get some help if every day is like today," she said.

"I have help." He motioned toward her then went back to typing.

"For today."

He gave her an odd look, as if he knew something she didn't, before pecking a few more keys then turning off the computer. He clapped his hands together once as he leaned back in his chair. "You as hungry as I am?"

Now that she thought about it, yeah, she had worked up an appetite. She thought of Mr. Brody's invitation and wished she could take him up on it. She'd love to catch up on everything that had happened in the years since she'd left. She'd wondered so many times since Chloe had never replied to her letters. But Natalie had to keep her distance until Chloe and Owen returned home.

"I could eat." That in itself was a miracle.

"Good, Sheila and I are taking you to dinner. You like Mexican?"

"That's not necessary." While she adored Dr. Franklin, the thought of small talk or, worse, deeper conversation freaked her out. What if she let something slip? What if through amazing powers of deduction, he figured out her real purpose for returning to Blue Falls? She knew she was stretching, but hiding in her motel room until the rest of the Brody clan came back from their trip seemed like the safest, wisest plan.

"I insist. You saved my bacon more than once over the past few days. It's the least I can do."

"Which I was glad to do. After all, if not for you I might be driving a delivery truck or scrubbing floors for a living."

Not that there was anything at all wrong with either of those jobs. They just weren't what spoke to her. She couldn't imagine ever getting up in the morning looking forward to delivering potato chips or mopping other people's floors. But each new day brought a new challenge in helping her animal patients feel better and live healthier lives. It made them happy, their owners happy, her happy.

"Somehow I doubt that. You had more drive than any little kid I'd ever seen. And the way the animals always responded to you, your path was meant to be."

She swallowed against the lump forming in her throat, one of gratitude this time. "That means a lot coming from you."

In the quiet that followed her words, Dr. Franklin's stomach growled audibly. He patted his middle. "I think we better get something to eat so my tummy doesn't do me in before I can retire."

Natalie couldn't think of a plausible reason to decline, so she followed Dr. Franklin the few blocks to La Cantina at the edge of downtown. He parked in the lot but she slipped into the end space on the side of Main Street.

The moment she spotted Sheila Franklin, it became more obvious just how much time had passed since Natalie's family fled Blue Falls. While Dr. Franklin didn't look all that much different from what Natalie remembered, his wife had aged more substantially. She was still a pretty woman for her age, but she was thinner and there was a look of not entirely well about her.

All that said, Sheila's smile was as wide and welcoming as it had ever been. She pulled Natalie into her arms for a stronger hug than Natalie would have guessed Sheila could give. Then the older woman stepped back and framed Natalie's face with her hands.

"Look at you. You've grown up into such a beautiful young woman."

Natalie blushed at the compliment. "Thanks. You look good, too."

Sheila stepped back, making a dismissive *pfft* sound. "No I don't, but you're sweet to say so. Had a little fight with some breast cancer last year, but I kicked its butt back to where it came from."

"I'm so sorry. I mean, I'm not sorry you kicked its butt. That I highly approve of."

Sheila laughed, and Natalie's heart lifted to hear Dr. Franklin's wife was on the mend. She hated the idea of him losing the woman he'd loved his entire adult life, the way Mr. Brody had lost his. Maybe Sheila's health scare was another reason he was so anxious to retire and move closer to their grandchildren.

"You okay, dear?"

Natalie realized her thoughts must have shown on her face when Sheila looked at her with concern.

"Yeah, fine."

"Let's take this chitchat inside," Dr. Franklin said. "I'm in dire need of some chips and salsa."

Sheila gave a little eye roll as she wrapped her arm through Natalie's and headed toward the front door of the restaurant. "The way he talks, it sounds as if I never feed the man."

Once they were seated and the waiter had taken their order, Dr. Franklin leaned his forearms against the table and looked right at Natalie.

"So, what do you think about taking over my practice and letting an old man retire?"

Chapter Six

Natalie was glad Dr. Franklin dropped his bomb before her hand made it to her mouth because she would have totally choked to death on a tortilla chip. She dropped the chip back into the basket.

"What?"

"I told you I've been thinking about retiring, and your arrival here seems like the perfect way for me to do that."

"Uh, I'm flattered, but there's one small problem. I live in Kansas."

"I'm sure they have moving vans in Kansas. And if Sheila and I relocate to the beach, our house would be available. See, perfect."

Maybe if they lived anywhere but Blue Falls. But after Natalie divulged her reason for being here to the Brodys, they weren't going to want to see her in town or have to depend on her to care for their animals when they needed veterinary care. Not to mention she wouldn't be able to look any of them in the eye and not be swamped with guilt by association.

"I appreciate the offer, I really do, but my job, my home, my family, they're all in Kansas. My life isn't in Blue Falls anymore." Even though a part of her irrationally wished it was, as if she'd left a part of herself behind here all those years ago and it sensed she had returned.

The skeptical look on Dr. Franklin's face made her want to squirm, tempted her to accept his offer even though it didn't make the smallest amount of sense. Yes, she'd dreamed of having her own practice where her schedule and decisions were hers alone, but it had never been anything more than that. She couldn't give up the security she had with her current job, not to follow some dream that might not work out. She remembered the feeling of not having enough money, of living on the edge of disaster, and she never wanted to experience that kind of worry ever again.

Natalie wanted to kiss the waiter for choosing that moment to bring them their food. It broke what felt like Dr. Franklin's laser-beam gaze directed right at her as if he could make her change her mind with sheer determination.

After the waiter left the table, Dr. Franklin sighed. "Well, the offer stands if you change your mind. But one way or another, I'm retiring soon and moving near my grandbabies before I'm too old to play with them."

Thankfully, Sheila steered the conversation toward less potentially life-altering topics for the duration of their dinner, and Natalie was finally able to relax enough to enjoy the evening.

When the waiter stopped by to clear away their empty plates, he asked if they wanted dessert. At the same moment, Dr. Franklin yawned.

"I think we'll pass," Sheila said. "Somebody's ready for bed."

"Don't let her fool you," Dr. Franklin said. "She just doesn't want me to get fat."

That drew a hoot from Sheila and a smile from the waiter before he headed to the kitchen with the dirty dishes. Natalie smiled, too, happy that she'd been able to spend time with the Franklins despite Doc putting ideas in her head that she wished he hadn't.

"What are you smiling at?" he asked when he noticed Natalie watching them.

"You two are cute together."

Doc and Sheila gave each other matching

looks of love and admiration as he wrapped his hand around his wife's.

"I was a goner the moment I laid eyes on her," he said.

His admission set off such an intense longing in Natalie that she wished there was some medicine she could take to make it go away. She glanced at Sheila in the same moment that the older woman looked at her. Sheila gave her a small smile of understanding, as if Natalie's feelings were as visible as the empty chip basket in the middle of the table.

"I hope you find a man who will be as good to you as Harry has been to me. You'll be a lucky woman."

An image of Garrett Brody popped into her mind, causing her to lower her gaze so she didn't reveal that tidbit, as well. She tried shoving his image out of her head, telling herself she had about as much chance with Garrett as she did with Michael Fassbender.

After saying good-night to the Franklins outside the restaurant, Natalie didn't think she could face shutting herself away in her little motel room yet. Nervous energy pulsed through her body as Dr. Franklin's offer bounced around in her head, bumping into images of Garrett and the knowledge of why she was in Blue Falls.

Hoping a walk would alleviate the jittery feelings, she headed up the sidewalk, pausing to look in shop windows in an effort to purge her mind of things that could not be.

She ended up in front of the Mehlerhaus Bakery. A woman close to Natalie's age opened the door, releasing the tantalizing scent of fresh-baked sweets into the evening air. Maybe a nice sugar high would occupy her mind with other thoughts for a while. Not to mention a pastry might make her taste buds happy.

When she stepped up to the counter a few minutes later, the woman on the other side of the display case gave her a curious look.

"Natalie?"

Surprised that someone recognized her, she nodded.

The other woman smiled. "I thought so. You resemble your mom, at least how I remember your mom looking."

Considering where she was standing, Natalie hazarded a guess at the other woman's identity. "Keri?"

"Yep. I heard you were back in town. Wow, it's been forever."

Damn, why hadn't she just gone back to the motel? The more people who knew she was in town, the more likely someone was going to start asking questions she couldn't answer, wouldn't answer for anyone but the Brodys.

"Yeah. I was glad to see the bakery still here."

Keri rested her arms against the top of the glass case. "Sort of in my blood. So, what can I get you?"

Natalie shifted her attention to the sugary confections on offer. "How does anyone ever make a choice? Everything looks delicious."

"It's part of my evil plan to make everybody buy one of everything."

Natalie laughed a little, and it alleviated a smidge of the tension that had been knotting her muscles all evening.

"Well, I don't think I have quite that much room in my stomach, but I'll take one of the lemon tarts."

As Keri reached into the case for the tart, she asked, "So, how have you been? I heard through the grapevine that you're a vet."

"Yeah, up in Kansas."

"It totally makes sense. I remember we brought in our puppy to see Doc Franklin when

I was young. He'd been bitten by a spider. I was crying, convinced he was going to die, and your mom assured me he'd be okay. And when they took Bucky into the back of the clinic, you said you'd keep him company. I still remember that as if it was yesterday."

Natalie had no recollection of that conversation, but it did sound like her mom. Even though she currently harbored conflicted feelings about her mother, Natalie knew that her mom had a good heart and had always loved animals of all kinds.

"I know she might not remember it, but tell her thank you for that from me."

Natalie nodded. "I will."

Before Keri brought up any other tales from the past, Natalie paid for her tart and turned to leave. She nearly dropped her dessert when she saw a man in a sheriff's department uniform step inside. She froze, unable to move or think clearly for what felt like the longest seconds in the history of time.

It occurred to her that she should let the local authorities know what her father had done. After all, Karen Brody's death was still sitting in their files classified as an unsolved… death. It wouldn't be classified murder, right? Her father hadn't meant to kill Karen. Vehicular manslaughter? It didn't matter what term was attached to the accident, the result was the same—a good person's life ended too soon.

The tacos she'd had for dinner churned in her stomach, making her wonder if she'd ever be able to eat without her stomach revolting again.

"Hey, Simon," Keri said. "You remember Natalie Todd, right? We went to elementary school together before her family moved."

The man in uniform took a few steps toward Natalie, making her grip the tart a bit too tightly. Before she squished it completely, she forced herself to relax her grip.

"Yeah." The man smiled as Keri rounded the end of the front counter. He lifted his arm and wrapped it around Keri's shoulders, making it obvious they were a couple. Wait, Simon?

"Simon Teague?"

"The one and only."

"You're a deputy?" Sure, it'd been a lot of years since she'd known Simon and his brothers, but the sight before her did not compute.

"Sheriff, actually."

"You're kidding." The words were out of Natalie's mouth before she could stop them.

Keri burst out laughing. "I know, right?"

"Not feeling the love right now," Simon said.

Keri placed her hand on his chest. "Just because I laugh doesn't mean I don't love."

"It's a good thing you're cute."

"And keep the sheriff's department supplied in doughnuts."

Simon rolled his eyes. "Woman, you're killing me."

That's when Natalie saw the ring on Keri's left hand. "You two are married?"

"Yeah," Simon said. "And a word of warning—if you stick around long enough, Verona Charles will match you up with someone, too."

Damn if Garrett's image didn't plunk itself down front and center again. Choosing to ignore it, she instead said, "Who?"

"Oh, you might not remember her," Keri said. "She's the aunt of a friend of ours who moved here after you left, and self-appointed town matchmaker. Thing is, she's pretty good at it, like she's got a sixth sense or something."

Whoever this Verona woman was, Natalie needed to steer clear of her. In fact, she needed to keep her distance from everyone until she could complete her mission and get the heck out of town.

She glanced at the department patch on the arm of Simon's uniform, promising herself that she'd tell him the truth about Karen's death before she left Blue Falls. But not before she told the Brodys. They shouldn't hear the truth from Simon or anyone other than her.

GARRETT EXAMINED PENELOPE'S WOUND, glad to see it was already beginning to heal with no signs of infection. Not only was Natalie Todd a beautiful woman, but she was also very good at her job.

His phone buzzed with a text message. He stepped out of Penelope's stall, closing the door behind him, before pulling the phone off his belt.

Owen had texted him a photo, one of him, Linnea, Chloe and Wyatt standing at the front of the cruise ship, a vast expanse of blue ocean behind them. They held a sign that read Don't You Wish You Were Here? Owen in particular looked as if he was rubbing it in.

Already plotting ways to get back at his siblings, he texted Owen back—a picture of a fresh pile of horse manure and Was just thinking of you.

Actually, he'd been thinking about Natalie, as he'd been doing much too often since they'd crossed paths at the music hall. No matter what was going on, he could usually lose himself in the never-ending ranch work. But that wasn't the case this time, and wasn't that just dandy considering she didn't seem to harbor the same interest toward him. What did he expect? Her life was two states away.

He'd considered texting Chloe that Natalie was back in Blue Falls, but something kept him from doing so. She didn't need to be thinking about anything that was going on here. His sister rarely took time for herself, so she deserved these days away with Wyatt. Even Owen, the little, taunting bastard, should be able to enjoy his honeymoon without thinking about the return of a childhood acquaintance from a time before they'd all lost their mother.

His dad strode into the barn, drawing Garrett back to the present.

"How's our patient doing?"

"Good." Garrett reached over the top slat of the stall and scratched Penelope between her ears. "Should be even better before Chloe gets back."

"That Natalie does have a way with animals. You ought to ask that girl out."

Garrett nearly choked as he shifted his gaze to his father. "You been hanging out with Verona?"

"Good Lord, no. That woman would probably try to match me up with somebody."

Garrett waited for the visceral rejection of that idea, but he was surprised when it didn't come. He'd loved his mom dearly, and it still hurt that she wasn't around to share in the big and small moments of all of their lives. But in that moment, Garrett realized that his father had been alone for a long time, most of Garrett's life.

"Would that be a bad thing?"

His dad looked at him as if he'd sprouted horns, but then the sharp edges of the expression smoothed out. "There was only one woman for me in this life."

"Sorry." Why the hell had he asked such a stupid question? He was beginning to think the ranch's water supply had been contaminated with something that was making his brain act abnormally.

His dad slapped the leather gloves he held in his right hand against his left palm. "No need to apologize." The awkward pause made Garrett want to kick himself. "I'm running into town to get some parts to fix the leak in the sink. Going to stop by the hospital to see Charlie Small. Damn fool fell off a ladder and broke his hip."

"What was he doing on a ladder?" Charlie Small, who'd worked at the feed store all of Garrett's life, had to be nearing eighty years old.

"His cat got on the roof, and he had the bright idea he could get him down. He's lucky he didn't break his neck."

After his dad left for town, Garrett started feeding the horses and mucking out stalls. He'd much rather be out moving the herd to new pasture, but he and his dad had decided to wait a couple more days before making the move. All he knew was that he needed to stay busy, try to occupy his mind with something other than Natalie Todd.

NATALIE WALKED ALONG the path through the cemetery, trying to remember where her grandparents' graves were located. She hadn't been here in so long that her memory was fuzzy. The image of a stone angel was the main thing she remembered, though she was pretty sure it wasn't part of her grandparents' gravestones. They hadn't been wealthy people, either.

She scanned the names as she walked by stones of all shapes, sizes and colors, amazed by the money that had been sunk into some of them. It wasn't a happy way to start her day, but it was somehow better than sitting in that motel room staring at four walls, especially since she'd had another horrible night of sleep and woke up irritable.

Her feet stopped moving when she saw the angel from her memories. It wasn't as big as she remembered and had weathered with the passage of years, but its outstretched hand still pointed the way to her destination.

As she passed the angel statuary, she took a moment to look at the name at the base. Mildred Canton, born 1861, died 1920. All these years Natalie had remembered the stone angel looking over Mildred but not the woman herself. She wondered if that's how everyone ended up when fate didn't direct them toward a life as president, pioneer or movie star. If you were a rancher, an alcoholic father who couldn't keep a job or a veterinarian from the Great Plains, did you end up just being a forgotten name at the base of a stone statue in some kid's foggy memories?

Natalie shook off the melancholy thoughts and walked the last few feet to her maternal grandparents' graves. She didn't have a lot of memories of Stephen and Lola Shaw, but a few snippets were enough to make her smile.

Grandpa Stephen holding her on his lap as she opened a Christmas present—a thousand-piece jigsaw puzzle, what she'd called a big-girl puzzle. Grandma Lola's homemade cinnamon rolls that had been as big as Natalie's dad's hand. Natalie might have only a few memories of her grandparents, but it would have felt wrong to return to Blue Falls and not visit them.

She crouched next to their simple stone and pulled up a few weeds that were creeping up around the edges. Then she placed the fresh flowers she'd just bought a few minutes earlier at the base of the gray granite.

"Hey, Grandma, Grandpa. I know it's been a long time." She felt silly talking to a rock, but it seemed she ought to say something instead of just staring at it. So she told the final resting place of her grandparents that her mom was okay, about what Allison and Renee were doing with their lives, that she was a vet and that she remembered the old beagle they used to have. Poor little blind, arthritic Pookie.

"Dad's gone now," she said, a lump forming in her throat. "Maybe…" Her voice faltered, and she had to swallow before continuing. "Maybe you could show him around."

She rose to her feet and took a deep breath, glad she'd done this despite the fact she'd had enough of visiting cemeteries lately. Her gaze drifted across the cemetery until it landed on the real reason she'd come here today. Feeling queasy, she headed up the hill toward Karen Brody's grave.

Seeing Karen's name on the rose-colored stone with Beloved Wife and Mother etched below punched Natalie right in the heart. More than two decades may have passed since Karen's death, but in that moment the pain of her loss was as fresh as the day she'd been laid to rest. Natalie would swear she could feel Chloe's small, sweaty hand squeezing hers.

With tears pooling in her eyes, she kneeled next to the grave and placed the bouquet of pink roses gently on the ground. Then she skimmed her fingertips over Karen's name.

"I'm so sorry," she whispered. "I'm so sorry my dad did this to you. I know he was sorry, too. I hope you can find it in your heart to forgive him."

Natalie realized she was addressing herself as much as Karen's spirit. Though she had no doubt her dad had been deeply regretful about what he'd done, she couldn't deny she was still angry that he'd run away, that he'd done so much damage and then been too much of a coward to confess. It would be so much easier if she could hate him, but she couldn't. Despite everything, she'd loved her dad even if she wanted to scream at him until she was hoarse. But she'd been denied even that because you didn't scream at a man who was taking the last breaths of his life.

The tears in her eyes overflowed, and she finally let go of all the sorrow and loss that had been eating away at her even before her dad's death.

She didn't know how long she cried, but it didn't matter. And if someone saw her sobbing over the grave of a woman who'd been gone for twenty years, she'd deal with it. Nothing could be harder to face than the task she'd been sent to Blue Falls to complete. Again, she questioned if she could go through with it, if she should. It seemed the Brodys were happy. Could she bring sorrow back into their lives?

Her phone rang, startling her. One didn't expect to hear a phone ringing in the middle of a cemetery. Thankful for the excuse to push hard questions and painful memories to the side, she pulled her phone out to see Doc Franklin's name on the display.

"Hey, Doc," she answered, trying to mask the remnants of her tears.

"I need a big favor," he said.

"If this is about me taking over your practice—"

"No, no. Although I still hope you change your mind about that. But I'm about to start a surgery and just got a call from the Burton ranch out at the edge of the county. They've got a bull that's not acting right. Can't even get him in a trailer to bring him in. Would you go check on him for me? At least do an initial assessment until I can get out there."

She wanted to refuse, suspecting that this might be another part of Dr. Franklin's plan to get her to stay in Blue Falls. But he really did sound harried, so she found herself agreeing. After all, it was better than watching the minutes tick away at an agonizingly slow pace.

"You're a lifesaver, sweetie."

Despite where she was and the fact tears were

still drying on her cheeks, she smiled. If she wasn't careful, he was going to wear her down even though there were so many reasons why that was a bad idea.

When she ended the call, her gaze fell on Mr. Brody's name next to his wife's. A chill ran down Natalie's spine. She'd always thought it was creepy to see a person's name on a headstone when they were still alive, almost as if it was tempting fate. An image formed in her mind of Wayne Brody sitting at his kitchen table eating pie, a smile on his face as he talked about Chloe's and Owen's weddings.

She couldn't do it. No matter what she'd promised her father, she couldn't break the Brodys' hearts all over again. Her dad would just have to understand. She would do this one last favor for Doc Franklin and then she'd head home, taking her awful secret with her.

Chapter Seven

Doc hadn't been kidding when he said the bull was in a bad mood. Natalie would swear she could hear the animal say, "Go ahead, make my day," as he stared at her.

"How long has he been like this?"

"We noticed it this morning."

She thought she detected a limp in the bull's rear right leg when he moved, but she needed to get closer to examine him. With the help of Mr. Burton and a couple of ranch hands, she tried to steer the angry bull from the corral to the chute that led toward the head gate. Each time they almost succeeded, the cranky bull eluded capture. But he seemed to be tiring, so maybe, just maybe, this next time would be the charm.

"We about got him," one of the ranch hands said.

The words were still echoing in Natalie's ears when the bull suddenly bucked away from the chute, straight toward her. She didn't even have time to think about moving. One moment she was facing a ton of angry bull, and the next she was on the ground with white-hot spears of pain shooting from her leg directly into her brain.

As she cried out, she somehow also heard the sound of hooves. Oh, God, she was going to be trampled. But in the next moment, three faces were staring down at her. She couldn't make out their features with the blazing sun above them.

"Lie still," said a voice, but the pulsing of the pain center in her brain prevented her from distinguishing which dark figure had uttered it. "Lennie, go call an ambulance."

Natalie opened her mouth to say she didn't need an ambulance, but what came out was a moan. Her vision dimmed at the edges, and she felt coated in sweat that was cold one moment and burning her skin the next.

For some reason, she started to lift the upper part of her body, but one of the men gently kept her on the ground.

"Don't move. Pretty sure you've broken your leg, and you've got a deep gash on your arm."

It wasn't until he pointed it out that Natalie realized that some of the pain she was experiencing was indeed coming from her right forearm. It felt as if it weighed as much as the bull when she lifted it. Bright red blood flowed down her arm, disappearing under the edge of her T-shirt and causing nausea to well in her stomach. She might have gone to vet school, but she couldn't stand to see her own blood.

It became harder to focus, and she blinked against blurry vision as she let her arm drop.

One of the guys touched the side of her face. "Come on, Doc. Stay with us."

But she didn't want to stay. She wanted, needed to go. Tears leaked out of the corners of her eyes, streaking down into her ears. Almost as painful as her injuries was the knowledge that she wasn't going home today. Her father's mistake had brought her back to Blue Falls. Now hers was trapping her here.

THE FIRST THING Natalie noticed as she started to wake was how dry her mouth was, as if someone had stuffed it with cotton balls. She licked her lips as she gradually opened her eyes. No one else was in the room, so she watched people walking by out in the corridor as the anesthetic fog slowly receded from her brain.

Gradually, the events of the morning came

back to her and she was able to think more clearly. She lifted her injured arm to see it wrapped in several layers of gauze and tape. No doubt there were several stitches underneath the bandaging. She punched the button to raise the head of the bed then folded back the blanket to reveal a cast reaching from her knee all the way down to her foot with only her toes peeking out. She closed her eyes and barely kept herself from crying out in frustration.

Damn it. Why had she allowed her dad to make her promise to come back here? Despite a few bright moments seeing people she'd once cared for, it had been a disaster from the minute she'd rolled into town.

Needing to do anything other than lie in her hospital bed, she lifted the head some more then eased her legs off the side. She spotted a set of crutches in the corner. If she could get to them, at least she'd be mobile and could get out of here. Even her room at the Country Vista Inn was better than a hospital room. It was true what they said about doctors being the worst patients, even if the doctor's patients were normally cows and horses.

Carefully, she slid her good foot down to touch the floor, flinching a little at the cold of the tile. When she managed to bring the other foot down, she grimaced against a dull ache. No doubt her leg was going to hurt a lot more when the meds wore off, so she needed to vacate the premises before that happened. Whoever had fixed her up might get the bright idea to keep her here. Maybe she could fly Allison down to drive her back to Kansas. She shook her head slowly. What a royal mess.

Movement outside the open door caught her attention. Someone walked by, but by the time it registered who it was, Wayne Brody was taking a couple of steps backward and meeting her gaze.

"Lord, girl, what happened to you?"

"A surly bull and I had a bit of a disagreement."

"I'm guessing you lost the argument."

"You could say that." She took a breath and tried to push herself to her feet. Her head swam enough to knock her off balance, and she teetered sideways.

Mr. Brody took a quick step forward and grabbed her uninjured arm. "Whoa, what do you think you're doing?"

"The plan was to get those crutches in the corner and put on some real clothes, then walk out of this place." The smells and sounds reminded her too much of the several times over the past few months that her dad had been in and out of the hospital. Being in her clinic was different—it didn't have the same feel of sickness and despair.

"Looks to me like you need to sit back down."

"Excellent advice," said a doctor in a white lab coat as he swept into the room.

Natalie knew when she was outnumbered, so she sat down but refused to lie back in the bed. The doctor stepped in front of her and crossed his arms.

"Trying to make a clean getaway, I take it?"

She noticed the teasing gleam in his eyes. "Something like that."

"I'm not opposed to dismissing you, but do you have someone to pick you up? Your identification said you are from Kansas. Or is that old information?"

"No, it's current."

"I'll give her a ride," Mr. Brody said. "I'm done here now anyway."

"Why are you here?" Natalie asked.

"Visiting a friend who isn't having any better of a day than you are."

She didn't like the idea of spending more time with Mr. Brody when her father's secret was still burning a hole inside her, but if it was the only way she could get out of the hospital, she was taking it. After all, it wasn't that far to the motel. She'd figure out the next step then.

After the doctor explained the extent of her injuries, he turned to Mr. Brody. "She should be fine to get around on her own in a couple of hours, but she'll need assistance if you have stairs."

Natalie opened her mouth to correct the doctor, but Mr. Brody spoke first. "Don't worry. We'll take good care of her."

No, no, no. She couldn't let this happen. "I'm fine, really. And there are no stairs at the motel."

"There's also no room service at the Country Vista," Mr. Brody said. "With Chloe and Owen out of the house now, we've got plenty of room."

"I can't impose."

Mr. Brody made a dismissive sound. "Impose? What are you talking about? You spent enough nights at our house when you were a kid that I began to think you were one of ours."

Natalie bit her lip and tried to slow her steadily increasing heart rate. There was no way she could stay under the Brodys' roof and not tell them. But then she couldn't tell them when she had no way of leaving.

"Please, I just need a ride to the motel."

"We'll go there to pick up your stuff. Now, no more arguing." He bopped the end of her nose as he had when she was a kid. He had made her giggle then, but now it only made her want to cry.

GARRETT SCOOTED OUT from under his truck just as he heard his dad turn into the driveway. He grabbed the shop rag and wiped the dark splatters from the oil change off his hands. When he glanced toward his dad's truck, he realized someone was with him. As his dad pulled past him, Garrett saw it was Natalie. His heart rate kicked up a notch before he scolded himself for that reaction.

Even though one part of him wanted to hightail it to the back of the ranch and stay there until Natalie left and another part really wanted to go immediately to her side, he did neither. Instead, he casually walked to the back of his truck, still wiping his hands, and leaned against the rear fender. Had Natalie been on her way to check on Penelope only to experience car trouble? Nothing else made any sense.

At least not until she opened the passenger

side door, revealing a thick bandage on her arm and a cast on her leg.

Garrett forgot his determination to act casual as he walked toward her. "What happened?"

His dad rounded the front of the truck. "She pulled a Wyatt this morning."

At her confused expression, his dad patted her on the shoulder. "Remember how I said Chloe met Wyatt?"

The lines on her forehead eased as if she made the connection.

"A bull did this?" Garrett asked.

His dad met his gaze. "Yep, out at the Burton place." He motioned Garrett forward. "Help me get her into the house."

"I can manage," Natalie said.

"You heard what the doc said. No stairs by yourself." He pointed toward the wooden steps that led up to the front porch.

Garrett couldn't help chuckling. Natalie leveled a narrowed look at him.

"I'm not laughing at you," he said. "Just at the fact that we've somehow become the newest getaway for people needing to heal."

It hit him suddenly that the last two people to occupy the guest room were now married to his siblings. With that track record… Nope, best not to think like that.

He stood at the ready as Natalie eased out of the truck. Garrett guessed by the size of the bandage on her arm that using crutches was going to be painful, so he stepped up to her side as his dad positioned himself on the other. Natalie placed her arms around their shoulders and allowed them to lift her. Garrett got a good whiff of some faint, feminine scent, vanilla with a touch of something he couldn't identify. He closed his eyes for a moment, giving himself a quick pep talk about how now wasn't the right time to be thinking about how he'd like to nuzzle Natalie's skin until he found the source of that scent.

"You know, if I had to tangle with a bull, I would have at least liked a chance at some prize money first," she said.

Garrett's dad barked out a laugh, and Garrett smiled.

But in the next moment, Natalie grunted in pain. Garrett glanced at her face in time to see the way she was pressing her lips together as if to keep from crying out. Unwilling to put her through any more than she'd already endured today, he swept her up into his arms.

Natalie gasped.

"Did I hurt you?" His eyes met hers, and he nearly gasped himself. Though it was the last thing he should be thinking about, his first thought was how sweet and pink her lips looked and how much he suddenly wanted to kiss them.

"Um, no, but put me down before you throw out your back."

He laughed at that. "Honey, it's going to take something a lot heavier than you to do that."

When Garrett reached the top of the steps, however, he realized his mistake. With all the weddings that had been going on lately, he couldn't avoid thinking about what carrying a woman across the threshold symbolized. And damned if the barely hidden smile on his dad's face didn't tell him that the same thought had occurred to him, as well.

Garrett chose to ignore it as well as Natalie's assertion that she could make it the rest of the way herself. Instead, he waited until his dad opened the front door then carried Natalie into the living room. But when he deposited her on the end of the couch, he had to fight the strange need to not let go of her. He forced himself to take a few steps away.

"Would you like something to drink?"

"Honestly, both of you, I can manage. I would have been able to manage at the motel."

His dad patted Natalie on the top of her head as he started toward the kitchen. "This one grew up stubborn."

Natalie Todd grew up to be a lot of things Garrett hadn't expected, including the reason that he suddenly needed to make himself scarce before he embarrassed himself as well as her.

As he headed down the hallway with the excuse that he needed to wash off the grease and dirt of the day, he wondered where their old tent was—because camping out under the stars by himself was looking like a really good idea right about now.

ABOUT AT THE end of what she could handle in one day, Natalie made the excuse that she was tired and would like to go lie down. Mr. Brody moved to help her, but she held up her hand.

"I appreciate it, I really do, but I can't depend on you all to help me every time I need to move. I know a ranch doesn't run itself. You and Garrett do what you need to, and don't worry about me. I promise not to tumble down the front steps."

"I do believe some of my kids rubbed off on you."

She managed a smile then reached for her crutches. Though pain shot up her arm when she put her weight on it, she forced herself not to show it. By the time she walked the short distance to the room that used to be Chloe's, she really was ready to rest. She needed to call Allison to get her out of this jam, but it'd be best to call when she was alone in the house. Maybe she'd just lie down and allow the pain throbbing in her arm and leg to settle down.

But as she snuggled into the bed, she realized she was more exhausted than she'd thought. Combined with the postsurgery drugs still in her system, she succumbed to sleep in what seemed like half a dozen breaths.

When she woke, it took her a moment to figure out why. And where she was.

"Natalie? Are you okay?"

She blinked a couple of times then realized it was Mr. Brody's voice coming through the door and that darkness had fallen outside.

"Um, yeah."

"Dinner's ready."

Her nap had evidently turned into several hours of sleep. "Okay. I'll be out in a minute."

She listened to the sound of floorboards creaking as Mr. Brody walked away before lifting to a sitting position on the side of the bed. She rubbed a hand over her face then back over her hair to smooth it. The movement sent a wave of throbbing pain through her arm, causing her to grit her teeth until it passed. She hated taking pain medicine, but if she had any hope of making it through dinner with Garrett and his father, she'd better take one of the pills that had accompanied her out of the hospital.

After swallowing it, she managed to push herself to her feet. With some awkward thunking of the crutches, she made her way to the kitchen. She stopped dead in her tracks when she spotted Garrett placing a plate of pork chops on the table. Gone were the dirty clothes he'd been wearing earlier, replaced by a snug gray T-shirt and clean jeans. He'd obviously taken a shower recently because his hair still looked damp. Heaven help her, he looked good enough to eat. She had the wholly inappropriate thought that she'd like to have him for dinner.

"I think the realization that you cooked dinner has struck our guest dumb, Garrett," Mr. Brody said with a laugh.

Garrett looked up at her then rounded the table. "How are you feeling?"

"Fine."

He lifted one dark eyebrow.

"Okay, like I got run over by a train. But the nap helped." Unable to maintain eye contact with him, she glanced at Mr. Brody. "Sorry I slept so long. I could have helped out."

"I think it's best that you rest up and heal. We're beginning to get used to doing things on our own. We depended on Chloe for too long."

Natalie sensed there was more to Mr. Brody's words, but she didn't give any indication that she'd noticed. Garrett pulled out a chair for Natalie, and she offered him a small smile of gratitude. Even though she couldn't allow herself to get too attached to Garrett, she had to admit the gesture gave her a warm feeling in her middle.

It was nothing like the thrill that had raced along all her nerves when he'd literally swept her up into his strong arms earlier and carried her into the house as if she weighed no more than a pup, but then she doubted anything would ever make her feel like that again. If she hadn't been so exhausted earlier, she had no doubt she would have lain in Chloe's old bed and replayed those few moments over and over in her mind. Probably best she'd fallen asleep so quickly.

As Natalie filled her plate with a pork chop, green beans and one of those store-bought dinner rolls she always associated with Thanksgiving, she searched for something to say that wouldn't open up a conversation she didn't want to have. Thankfully, Mr. Brody saved them all from the awkward quiet.

"So before the Burtons' bull injured you,

were you able to figure out what was wrong with him?"

She realized that with everything that had happened since she'd awakened at the hospital, she hadn't even thought about the answer to that question. "No, didn't get a chance."

Garrett nabbed a roll, and her eyes focused on the length of that strong, tanned arm, wondering what it would feel like pulling her close.

"Oh, I talked to Doc Franklin late this afternoon," Garrett said, drawing her attention away from his sinewy arm up to his handsome face. "He said they found a piece of glass at the top edge of his hoof."

"Glass?"

"Yeah. Some people seem to think it's fun to throw beer bottles at fence posts. Sometimes the glass ends up in the edge of cattle pastures."

"That's horrible." Her hand tightened on her fork as she imagined the senseless danger that posed not only to herds but to horses and the ranch hands who worked the land.

The conversation drifted to the state of the Brodys' ranch, including Owen's horse-training business and the fact that they were going to be moving the herd to a new pasture over the next couple of days.

"You sure you'll be okay here by yourself?" Mr. Brody asked.

"I promise."

She popped the last of her roll in her mouth and chewed slowly, surprised and a little annoyed by how tired she was again, even after all the sleep she'd gotten that day. Maybe she was still catching up for all the days when she'd barely been able to string two hours of sleep together at any one time.

After wiping her mouth on her napkin, she looked at Garrett. "That was good."

He smiled, causing her heart to beat out of rhythm for a moment.

"Don't sound so surprised."

"We're not going to get our own cooking show anytime soon, but we get by," Mr. Brody said.

"Want some dessert?" Garrett asked.

Though part of her brain was screaming at her to go back to the bedroom before the sight of Garrett caused her to start drooling like a bloodhound, she said, "Sure."

She forced herself to focus on her cuticle so she wouldn't watch every move Garrett made. At least she tried. She sneaked a peek in time to see him reach into a cabinet. Damn, his jeans fit him nicely. How on God's green earth was that man not married with half a dozen gorgeous kids following him around the ranch?

Natalie jerked her gaze away from Garrett's rear right before he closed the cabinet and turned back toward the table. It took her a moment to realize what he was carrying. When he placed the box on the table, she stared at it for a moment before meeting his gaze.

"You've got an excellent bakery in town, and you have Twinkies snack cakes for dessert?"

He shrugged. "I had a coupon."

For a suspended moment, she just stared at him as if she couldn't have heard him correctly. And then she burst out laughing.

It felt better than anything had in weeks.

Chapter Eight

Natalie's unexpected burst of laughter caused an equally unexpected filling of Garrett's heart. She'd offered a small smile here and there since her return to Blue Falls, but this was the first time she'd actually looked and sounded happy. That he'd caused it, well, it made him feel strange, but in a good way.

Still, he wasn't about to let the laughter at his expense go unanswered.

"What's so funny?"

Natalie held up a hand. "Sorry. I'm just having trouble picturing the big, tall cowboy clipping coupons."

He crossed his arms and fixed his gaze on her, trying to look annoyed despite the fact that all he could think was that she was so damn beautiful.

"Well, big, tall cowboys have to watch the bottom line to keep ranches afloat."

She reined in her laughter, and the loss of it and the dimming of her smile made him want to throttle himself.

"Sorry. I understand about being careful about finances."

Of course she would. Granted, he hadn't paid a lot of attention to her when they'd been kids. But he did remember her family hadn't had much. Despite the years that had passed, one memory did stand out. It had been Christmastime, and his parents had gotten Natalie the same toy horse they'd gotten Chloe. He remembered seeing tears in her eyes, but at the time he hadn't understood why someone would cry over getting a toy. He'd probably thought she was just being a silly girl. But now he saw the entire scene from a grown-up perspective and hoped he hadn't said something stupid.

"What he's not telling you," his dad said, "is that Chloe made us both go through what she called Household Boot Camp as if we were going to starve and walk around stark naked if she didn't teach us how to get by without her."

"And coupon clipping was part of that," Natalie said. "I've got to say, the image of this is pretty awesome in my head."

His dad chuckled, and Garrett found himself just wanting to sit down and watch Natalie smile. Good Lord, his brain was addled. He slid into his seat and snatched a Twinkie, ripping it open while making himself stare at the package instead of her.

"What was worse than coupon clipping was how to make beds."

Natalie shuddered. "Because why make a bed when you're just going to get back in it, right?"

He looked up at her with what had to be an expression of surprise. "Exactly. But don't let Chloe hear you say that."

She smiled at him, and damned if he didn't feel it all the way down to his toes. He wanted to curse when he remembered that she was here only temporarily.

"So, Natalie, we typically just watch TV at night, but we've got some movies if you want to watch one," his dad said.

Natalie shifted her gaze away from Garrett. "Actually, I'm still pretty tired, so I'm going to turn in. But the TV won't bother me if you all want to watch it. Don't worry about me."

She scooted her chair back and reached for her crutches before Garrett could hop to her aid, and maybe that was a good thing. There was no reason to act overeager or let himself get any more interested in her.

His dad, however, did stand. "Is there anything you need?"

Natalie settled her weight on the crutches and smiled at his dad. "No, I'm fine. Thank you for dinner."

"That was Garrett's doing. He was a better study in that department than me."

Natalie shifted her gaze to him, and he'd almost swear there was a layer of nervousness in her smile. Did he make her nervous? Was it possible that she found him as attractive as he did her?

"Thanks," she said.

"You're welcome."

And with that she turned and clunked her way toward the hallway. Only when she disappeared from sight did he relax. He hadn't even realized he'd been tensed.

"For someone who prides himself on not showing his feelings, you sure are terrible at hiding them."

Garrett jerked his gaze toward his dad, probably too fast. "What's that supposed to mean?"

"You know exactly what it means. You also know playing dumb doesn't work with me. Thought you learned that lesson when you were no taller than my knee, about the time Owen ended up with a black eye."

Garrett sighed and shook his head once before standing and grabbing the box of Twinkies. "Doesn't matter."

"Of course it matters."

He shoved the Twinkies into the cabinet where they kept snacks that were easy to grab on the way out the door. "No, really, it doesn't, not when I have no intention of leaving Blue Falls and she's got a life in Wichita."

"Time will tell."

Garrett didn't respond, unwilling to keep the conversation going. His dad had never interfered in his kids' love lives before Chloe met Wyatt. But as soon as it was obvious those two were falling for each other, Wayne Brody suddenly got a lot more interested in marrying his offspring off. He wasn't as bad as Verona Charles, thank goodness, but Garrett still didn't need a matchmaker. Or someone pointing out what he already knew, that he was really attracted to Natalie Todd.

BY THE TIME Natalie woke the next morning, she could tell from the quiet of the house that she was alone. She glanced at the clock and realized that Garrett and his dad were probably already out moving the herd between pastures. She wished she were able to help, but she'd be more of a hindrance than anything in her condition.

But she had to get out of their house. The longer she stayed under their roof, the worse she was going to feel. And now she couldn't even tell them the truth if she wanted to, not until she had a way back to town. She was beginning to wonder what she'd done in a previous life to deserve the cascade of awfulness that had overrun her lately.

It hasn't all been awful.

True. There had been some nice moments with Garrett and his dad, ones she was going to treasure after she told them the truth and went home. Her heart ached when she thought about how much she would miss Wayne's fatherly warmth and the buzzy thrill she felt anytime she was near Garrett. It was as if that crush she'd had on him as a girl had continued to grow without her knowledge over the years and made itself known when they'd crossed paths again.

How she wished she had returned to Blue Falls under different circumstances. But she hadn't.

After a clumsy bath, she got dressed and made her way to the kitchen, intending to toast a couple of pieces of bread. But when she walked into the room, she saw a box and note in the middle of the table.

Thought you might like something from the "excellent bakery." Coffee is ready to go in the coffeemaker. Don't fall down the stairs. We'll be too tired to pick you up when we get back. —G

Natalie laughed and realized it was the second time Garrett had really made her laugh in less than a day. She couldn't believe he'd gone into town to buy her breakfast from the bakery before heading out to work. But what really made her smile more than the thoughtful gesture or his humorous command to not fall down the stairs was the smiley face he'd drawn next to the *G*. Garrett Brody didn't seem like a smiley face kind of guy, so it scared and excited her at the same time that he'd thought to leave those few strokes of the pen. But as she ran her thumb over that simple drawing, a heavy sadness descended on her.

She set the note aside and opened the box. Her mouth dropped open when she saw the two huge cinnamon buns inside. They weren't her Grandma Lola's, but the scent of cinnamon brought back fond memories anyway. How odd that she'd so recently been thinking about her grandmother's sweet specialty and then to be presented with these.

As she stared at the cinnamon rolls, she marveled at how easily she was falling back into place with old friends. Though it made her heart ache even more, she knew she had to stop the slide before she fell too far. While Garrett and Wayne were away from the house, she would call her mom and arrange to go home. She'd explain to her mother that she simply couldn't shatter the Brodys' lives all over again, that they would just have to live without the knowledge of what her father did. Natalie would have to find a way to forgive herself for lying to her dying father.

But first she had to feed her growling stomach. And try to convince herself that she wasn't delaying making the call because some part of her wished she could stay here.

With a shake of her head, she grabbed one of the cinnamon rolls and made her way to the microwave in a less-than-graceful fashion, flicking on the coffeemaker along the way. She stared out the window over the sink while the coffee brewed, enjoying the simple, sloping view up toward the back of the ranch. How many times had Karen Brody stared out this same window? How many times had Chloe, Owen and Garrett missed seeing her in this spot and so many others in their lives?

She closed her eyes and took a couple of slow, deep breaths, needing to hold it together until she could leave the ranch. She should have been more forceful with Wayne when he'd insisted she come home with him, but she'd been drugged up and not at her best. Plus, what was she going to do? Threaten him with a whack from one of her crutches?

When the coffee finished brewing, she poured herself a cup and programmed the timer on the microwave for ten seconds. By the time she managed to get her cup to the table, the cinnamon roll was warm. A few more awkward movements and she finally sat down with her breakfast, tired from simple tasks she wouldn't normally even think about.

The first bite made her moan in appreciation as the tangled flavors of cinnamon, sugar and butter flowed over her tongue. "Man, that's good," she said out loud.

She used the single-minded focus that she normally employed when she was working on a patient to keep other thoughts at bay so she could fully enjoy the cinnamon roll and the cup of coffee. As she finally ate the last bite, she had to admit that Keri's cinnamon rolls were almost enough reason by themselves to move back to Blue Falls.

But there were so many others why she should leave.

Knowing she couldn't put it off any longer, Natalie first washed her dishes then went to the guest room to get her phone. But before placing the necessary call, she made her way out to the porch. Though it was quite warm already, she much preferred the fresh air than being stuck inside. For as long as she could remember, she'd been an outside person. Give her a hiking trail over a gaming system any day.

Keeping in mind Garrett's instructions not to get near the front steps, she instead plunked down into one of the matching rocking chairs. Having evidently heard the door open, the two basset hounds came waddling out of the barn and straight toward the porch. They scrabbled their way up the steps and came to sniff at her exposed toes.

"Hey there, fellas." She reached down to scratch first one and then the other between the ears. They both seemed to love the attention. But when they toddled over to the edge of the porch at the top of the steps and plopped down, she finally placed the call to her mom.

But when the call went to voice mail, she was forced to leave a message. Not wanting to get into details, she simply asked her mom to call her back.

After ending the call, she stared out across the landscape. What was she supposed to do now? Maybe her mom was at work already and was busy with a customer. But when her mom still hadn't returned the call after an hour, she tried again. Still no answer. Trying not to be too concerned, she hit Allison's number.

"Hey, I was just about to call you," her sister said in answer.

"Oh. Is Mom okay?"

"Yeah, she's fine. I actually just talked to her."

"Really? I haven't been able to reach her."

The slight pause before Allison spoke again caused a knot of worry in Natalie's stomach despite her sister's assertion their mom was fine.

"That's because she's on a plane."

"A plane?" Could her mom be headed to

Texas even without knowing about Natalie's injuries?

"Uh, yeah. She's flying to Paris with Renee. We decided she deserved a vacation, a real one."

Natalie sat not knowing what to say. She honestly couldn't imagine her mom on a plane, let alone one flying to France. The only reason she even had a passport was because she had won a weekend in Cancun through a promotion at work a few years ago. In the next moment, a feeling of being pushed away swept over Natalie.

"When did she make this decision?"

"We talked her into it yesterday."

"And no one called to tell me?" She realized her voice sounded sharp, but this unexpected news was just one more thing throwing her for a loop.

"Mom said you were taking some time alone, that we shouldn't bother you."

Natalie leaned her head back and closed her eyes. "How much did this cost? I'll get my share to you and Renee." Despite the fact she was already bleeding money that she hadn't planned to spend on this trip to Texas.

"That's not necessary."

"What? Of course it's necessary. You've got a family, and I doubt Renee is rolling in money."

"And you've helped Mom and Dad a lot over the years, more than you ever told me or Renee. It's our turn."

She still didn't feel right about her sisters footing the entire bill of a trip for their mom, but she knew from the tone of Allison's voice that arguing further wouldn't do her any good.

"I hope she likes it."

"Renee thinks she will. And…though she'd never admit it, I think Renee feels guilty for running so far away. She needs to do this for Mom."

"Okay." She paused, imagining her mom seeing so many things for the first time. "Though I'd pay good money to see Mom staring up at the Eiffel Tower."

"Yeah."

Neither of them spoke for a moment, and Natalie figured her sister was thinking along the same lines—that their mom deserved this vacation, that maybe it would help her through the early days of her grief. Seeing the beauty of Paris was so much better for her than coming home to an empty house.

"So where are you?"

Allison's question caught Natalie off guard, though it shouldn't have. "Just on a road trip. Been a while since I've had some time off, too."

"This have anything to do with the argument you had with Dad the night he died?"

Hell, what was she supposed to say to that? She hated lying to her sister, but there was no reason to burden anyone else with the truth of what her father had done all those years ago.

"That was…a disagreement about how he handled things, but we got it out and over with. When he—" Natalie's throat filled with a twisted ball of sorrow, regret and a myriad of other emotions. "We'd come to an understanding before he was gone."

"You sure that's it? Because Mom acted weird, as if she knew what was going to happen before it did."

"Al, please trust me and let it go. There's been too much holding on to stuff that can't be changed."

Allison didn't immediately respond, and the few seconds of dead air made Natalie's nerves clench.

"Okay. I won't mention it again."

"Thank you."

They chatted for a few more minutes before Allison had to go. When Natalie clicked the End button on her phone, she realized just how stuck she was unless she flat out demanded Wayne or Garrett take her back to town. And that would result in the very questions she wanted to avoid.

"WHAT ARE YOU DOING?"

Natalie yelped and teetered sideways. But before she could fall, Garrett leaped into the laundry room and grabbed her around the shoulders. Without thinking, she allowed her gaze to meet his. And it was close, so very close. Her heart tossed in a few extra beats while her breath got lost on its way out of her lungs. She didn't think she'd ever wanted anything as much as she wanted to kiss him in that moment.

As if he'd seen her thought, he righted her

then took a couple of steps back. Even without him touching her, she could still feel his strong, warm arm wrapped around her, preventing her from damaging herself further.

"Thanks," she muttered and smoothed one of the towels she'd been folding.

"Why are you doing our laundry?"

She leaned her weight against the dryer. "Because I was bored out of my mind, and I'm not exactly a daytime-TV kind of person." She glanced up at him. "I can't just sit around doing nothing."

She expected an argument. Instead, he leaned one very nicely formed forearm against the doorjamb and nodded. "I get that."

"You do?"

"Yeah. I'm a terrible sick person, as well."

"I'm not sick."

"Invalid, whatever."

She saw a twinkle of mischief in his eyes and pitched a pair of socks at him.

He caught them midair, and the moment his fingers curled around the fabric she found herself jealous of a pair of socks.

"You okay?" he asked.

"Yeah. Why?"

He shrugged. "You got a funny look on your face."

Great, now she had to worry about projecting her attraction toward him across her face like a movie. As if she didn't have enough to hide from him. That thought doused the flame he'd stoked in her with his nearness. Why the hell did she have to be so physically attracted to him? She found herself wishing he'd do or say something that would make her like him less.

This time, she was the one to shrug and went back to folding washcloths.

"Make you a deal," he said, stepping closer again. "You fold, and I'll put away."

Needing him out of the confined space so she could breathe normally, she said, "Deal."

They ended up working well together, which should have made her happy but ended up frazzling her nerves even more. She wished with every cell in her body that the big, horrible secret didn't lie between them. But because it did, everything she did or said felt like another layer of lies.

When they were done with the laundry, she glanced into the living room. "So where's your dad?"

"He ran into town to get some pizzas from Gia's."

"I could have made something here."

"Don't worry about it. We'll use any excuse to order Gia's."

"Really? Figured you two would be more steak and potatoes kind of guys."

"We are. But there's room for pizza, too. And tacos. We could use a good Chinese place."

She laughed a little. "So basically, anything that's food."

"No. Nothing weird."

"So I shouldn't have Renee ship you some escargot from France?"

He gave her a look as if she'd lost her mind. "What do you think?"

"Personally, I think it'd be funny."

"Ugh."

She couldn't help but smile.

When she went to bed a couple of hours later, she was still smiling. She knew she should feel guilty about it and how much she enjoyed spending time with Garrett and his dad, but she wanted, just for a little while, to bask in the feeling. Because if Garrett somehow found out why she was in Blue Falls, those smiles on Garrett's face that made her melt inside were going to be replaced by pain and anger.

She made her way to the bedroom window and opened it so she could hear the sounds of the night. Before she really thought about what she was doing, she was leaning on the edge of the window and looking up at the sky, sending up silent prayers. They weren't even filled with words but rather feelings. She desperately wanted some way for everything to be…right. But that would take a miracle indeed.

Chapter Nine

Garrett normally slept pretty solidly through the night, so he was surprised when his eyes popped open right before two in the morning. A thump from the front of the house had him rolling out of bed and slipping on a pair of shorts. He opened his door as quietly as he could and eased up the hallway. When he saw the door to Chloe's old room was open, he realized Natalie must be up. He took a couple more steps and noticed her trying to open the front door.

"Are you okay?"

She looked back at him over her shoulder. "Oh, uh…I'm sorry. I didn't mean to wake you."

He waved away her concern. "Where are you going?"

She turned halfway toward him and gave him a sheepish look. "To watch a meteor shower."

"There's one tonight?"

"Yeah, it's supposed to be peaking soon. But I'm sorry I woke you up. I tried to be quiet."

"Don't worry about it. You know, I haven't seen a meteor shower in years." He headed toward her, and he thought he saw her eyes widen then flick downward for a moment before she turned back toward the door.

He glanced down at himself, at the fact that all he was wearing was a pair of shorts. Had that been interest he'd seen in her eyes? His heart beat a little faster at that thought, despite all common sense. Still, he couldn't prevent a smile from tugging at his lips as he moved closer to Natalie, reaching past her to open the door. When he put his hand at the small of her back to steady her, she stiffened the same way she had when he'd kept her from falling in the laundry room.

Maybe his attraction was reciprocated after all.

"Thanks," she said then rushed out the door a little more quickly than he'd seen her move on those crutches before. Either she was getting better with them or she was putting distance between them as fast as she could. A mischievous streak that didn't come out very often made him want to close that distance just to see her squirm.

It didn't take long for him to catch up to her since she could go no farther than the top of the steps. She stared up into the sky, seeming to ignore the fact he was even there.

Choosing to not think about the main reason he shouldn't let himself like Natalie any more than he already did, he stepped up beside her.

"We'd have a better view out from under the porch."

"This is okay," she said, keeping her gaze fixed on the sky. "Oh, there's one." As she pointed, she wobbled a little bit but caught herself before he could steady her.

Undeterred, he moved to the step in front of her, putting them face-to-face. "Give me your crutches."

"What?"

He pointed to one crutch then the other.

"I'm fine here."

"Are you afraid of me?"

Her forehead wrinkled. "No. Why?"

"Then stop being so contrary and come watch some meteors with me."

She exhaled in obvious frustration. "You sure did grow up to be bossy."

"Comes from being the oldest sibling. I bet if we asked your sisters, they'd say you're bossy, too."

"You are way too quick with the comebacks at this time of night." She shook her head. "If I'm coming down the steps, I need the crutches. Just catch me if I do a header."

"You don't need these," he said as he eased the crutches out from under her arms and leaned them against the edge of the porch.

"Garrett, don't you dare—"

Her words were cut off in a squeal of surprise as he scooped her up into his arms. "Shh. You don't want to wake up my dad, do you?"

"Then put me down."

"I will," he said as he turned and started walking toward where he'd parked his truck.

She turned her face away with a huff, which only served to make him smile.

When he reached the truck, he placed her on the opened tailgate then sat beside her. "See," he said as he pointed to the sky. "Much better view."

Just then, a meteor streaked across the sky.

"Okay, I'll give you that," she said.

"Do you suppose we get a wish for each one, or does that only apply when there's just one?"

"Not sure it matters."

He glanced at her, trying to judge by her profile why she sounded so…*sad* wasn't really the right word, but he couldn't place the exact emotion. All he knew was that his sister would be as fascinated by the "magic" of a meteor shower now as she'd been as a kid. It seemed that Natalie had left some of her childlike wonder far behind. He wondered why, but he didn't feel right about asking. They barely knew each other, and when she left Blue Falls this time, who knew if he'd ever see her again.

Not wanting to think about that or why he didn't like the possibility, he shifted his gaze to the sky.

WITH EACH METEOR that streaked across the heavens, Natalie silently thought about all the things she'd wish for if that kind of power existed.

That Natalie and her family had never left Blue Falls.

That her father had been able to kick his drinking problem.

That Karen Brody was still alive.

And that as she sat out under the stars with Garrett Brody, she could enjoy it.

Part of her ached to use the cloak of darkness to tell him the truth. Things were easier to say in the dark, right? But she just couldn't. He might not be married and off on a Caribbean cruise with his significant other, but he seemed happy enough. She didn't know if she could go through the rest of her life knowing that she'd ruined that happiness, that every time he thought of her he'd feel nothing but anger and heartache and betrayal.

"You're not watching the meteors," Garrett said.

"Huh?" she asked as she glanced over at him.

He pointed toward the sky, and that's when she realized she must have been staring out into the darkness of the surrounding rangeland. "Guess I'm more tired than I thought."

"You sure that's it?"

She fixed her gaze on her cast, cursing it and how it prevented her from making a hasty exit from her current situation.

"Yeah." She knew her answer sounded weak and not entirely truthful, but it was the best she could muster. Sitting so close to Garrett made it hard for her to think.

Garrett slid off the tailgate. "I'll take you back in."

She reached out and grabbed his arm. "No, it's okay. We can wait until it's over."

He captured and held her gaze. "You said you're tired."

She fought the burning need to lower her gaze to that amazing chest of his. "I'll sleep later. This meteor shower doesn't come around very often."

He stared at her in a way that made her feel as if he was picking through the layers of her brain. And then she watched as his eyes lowered for a moment to her lips. How she wished she could lean forward, invite him to do more than look at her lips. His mouth parted, and her breath caught as she waited for him to speak. Instead, he closed his mouth and leaned back against the tailgate.

The longer they sat and watched the celestial show, the more Natalie found herself relaxing. It didn't make any sense considering nothing had changed between them. And it only served to make her wish even harder for things she couldn't have, such as being able to sit under the stars with Garrett, hold his hand, maybe even have him put his arm around her. But this would be all she'd have, so she made up her mind to soak up every moment of this quiet time together.

Gradually, the meteors came further and further apart. The silence of the night was broken by Garrett yawning. She looked over at him.

"I'm sorry for keeping you out here. You need to sleep."

Garrett shifted to face her. "Don't apologize. I enjoyed this."

A couple of moments ticked by as he watched her, as she wondered what it would feel like if she placed her palm against his cheek. She imagined his warm skin, stubble that he would shave away in a few hours.

"Me, too," she finally said, realizing she meant it despite the stress of the secret she carried. For a moment, she imagined telling him the truth and having him understand how hard it was for her, that they would hold each other as they both grieved their losses.

Knowing it was nothing more than a fantasy, she broke eye contact.

"Guess we should both get some more beauty sleep," he said. In the next moment, he lifted her into his arms again and carried her back to the porch.

Natalie wondered if he could feel how fast her heart was beating, but there was no way she could control it. As he crossed the distance to the porch, a very lonely part of her allowed herself to imagine him carrying her as effortlessly to bed then joining her there. Even if she could be with him only once, she wished with all her heart she could have that memory to cling to.

When he reached the top of the steps, he lowered her gently to her feet but didn't immediately let go. For a long moment, his hand stayed at her waist and she looked up at him. Panic bloomed to life in her brain, demanding she say something before she made a horrible mistake and invited him to kiss her.

"Thank you," she said.

Despite the darkness, she'd swear she saw something change in his eyes. But before she could even begin to figure out what it was, he nodded then bent to retrieve her crutches. He didn't meet her eyes again as he held the door open for her or as she made her way as quietly as she could into the living room.

When he didn't follow, she glanced over her shoulder. "Good night, Garrett."

"Good night."

The heaviness returned to her heart as she made her way back to the guest room. As she sat on the side of the bed, she couldn't help the tears that pooled in her eyes. But this time they weren't for her father or Karen Brody. These tears came from the part of her heart that wished it could love Garrett Brody.

GARRETT TOOK HIS time letting the horses out into the corral so they could get some exercise. He didn't want Natalie to know that he was watching her, making sure she didn't fall and break another bone.

After their night of watching the meteor shower, she'd been quiet at breakfast and hadn't met his eyes once. When he'd seen her outside, making her way awkwardly down the driveway, his heart had leaped into his throat until his dad had said she'd come out through the back door. Thankfully that way she had to navigate only one small step instead of the steep ones in the front.

So he'd fed the horses and mucked the stalls while his dad conducted business on the phone. All the while, Garrett listened for any hint that Natalie might need help. When he managed to move to where he could see her, the tight, clenched-teeth look on her face told him just how painful using crutches on the uneven ground must be for her. But based only on the few days she'd been back in Blue Falls, he'd figured out that Natalie was not a woman used to just sitting around doing nothing. In that they were alike, which just made him like her more.

"When are you going to cave and ask that girl out?"

Garrett sighed then slowly looked at where his dad was leaning against the top rail of the corral. There was no sense trying to lie and say he wasn't interested in Natalie.

"Not a good idea."

"I disagree."

"You're entitled to your opinion." Forcing himself not to look toward where Natalie was making her way back toward the house, Garrett returned to the barn to saddle his horse so he could go look for a few stragglers they'd missed while moving the herd.

His dad followed him. "All I'm saying is that sometimes you have to grab the opportunities life places in front of you because they might not come again."

Garrett knew his dad was thinking of the wife he'd lost, the mother who would have been beaming at Chloe's and Owen's weddings had she lived.

He didn't respond to what his dad said, but he couldn't get it out of his head the whole day he was out riding the acre upon acre that had been passed down through the Brody generations. He even allowed himself to think about providing a new generation, but that seemed so far out of reach. He'd thought he'd seen a flicker of interest in her eyes the night before, but he'd also felt the deliberate distance she placed between them, as well. Maybe she realized, as he did, that getting involved would be a bad idea. Or perhaps she had someone back home. That thought made him squeeze his reins until his knuckles turned white.

He pulled to a stop along a gentle rise in the landscape. As he scanned the area for the last of the stragglers, his thoughts settled back on Natalie. Away from her, he was able to concentrate more. Though she was friendly enough, his gut told him that something heavy weighed on her thoughts. She did her best to hide it, but sometimes he'd swear he could feel tension coming off her like heat from flames.

Maybe she was just mourning her father. He knew from experience that people mourned their losses in different ways. He and his siblings were prime examples of that. He wished he was one of those people who was good at talking about feelings, but that wasn't his domain. He supposed he was a stereotypical guy, keeping most of that kind of stuff to himself.

Movement in the distance proved to be his renegade cow. Glad to have something to pursue that he knew how to deal with, he set off down the hill.

An hour later, he made his way back toward home. When he walked into the barn leading his horse, he was surprised to see Natalie standing next to Penelope's stall, her forehead leaning against the mare's.

She jerked her head up at his approach, the sudden movement causing Penelope to toss her head, as well. Natalie quickly moved to soothe the animal, rubbing her hand down the horse's face and talking to her in a soft voice that also drew Garrett closer.

"Looks like you're getting around better," he said.

"Yeah. Next thing you know, I'll be starting a crutch 5K."

He laughed, happy that she seemed to be in a good mood. "That has a lot of comic potential."

She snorted then laughed when Penelope did the same.

He went about removing his horse's saddle and tack, checking the hooves for any rocks, then giving him feed and fresh water. Garrett half expected Natalie to vacate the barn before he finished, but when he stepped out of the stall, she'd moved to a different spot in front of one of Owen's horses.

"You trying to charm all the horses?"

She grinned at him, and his stomach performed an unexpected cartwheel.

"Maybe."

"You want to go for a ride?" The words were out of his mouth before he realized his brain had even formed them.

She thunked the side of her cast with one of the aluminum crutches. "Don't think that's in my immediate future."

Damn it, he wasn't giving up that easily. Whether his dad's words from that morning had wormed their way into his brain or he'd just finally decided to toss all common sense, he didn't know. But he was going with it, at least until he got totally and utterly shot down.

"We can make it work."

"You just got in from all day in the saddle."

"And I suspect you've been on enough ranches to know that the fact there is a good amount of daylight left means this isn't anywhere near the longest day I've put in on horseback. Plus, riding with a pretty gal is a lot more fun than chasing ornery cows."

He'd swear he saw her cheeks redden before she turned away. It was all the encouragement he needed to grab his gear and saddle up Sophie, one of their gentlest horses.

"Garrett, really, you don't have to go to all this trouble."

"It's no trouble."

She sighed. "You really are stubborn."

"I think you might have mentioned that before."

She shook her head, but it was accompanied by a small smile that made him ridiculously happy.

He hurried to ready Sophie and guided her over to the mounting block. Then he nodded for Natalie to come over.

"This feels like a terrible idea," she said, but

she made her way over to him anyway, taking a moment to let the horse nuzzle her palm.

"I won't let you fall off. And if it hurts too much, we'll come right back. But I'd venture a guess you're going stir-crazy."

She met his gaze, and something flickered in hers. Appreciation, maybe? Gratitude?

He held her hand as she made her way up the steps of the mounting block, ready to catch her should she stumble. But with a determined look on her face, she made it to the top. The problem came when she went to mount the horse. The grunt of pain from her as she tried to maneuver her broken leg over the horse's back made him want to kick himself.

"Wait," he said as he squeezed her hand. He stuck his foot in the stirrup and mounted. "Here, ride sideways in front of me."

At the look of concern on her beautiful face, he ran his thumb across the back of her hand as if it were a natural response. "I promise, you won't fall."

Part of him wondered if her concern stemmed from a fear of further injury or something else entirely. And as he eased her down in front of him and he secured his arms around her, he wondered if her concern was valid. Because having Natalie nestled that snugly next to him was going to have an effect, one he was going to be very lucky if she didn't notice.

Trying to focus on anything but the fruity scent of her hair, how closely his arm came to the swell of her breasts, and how tight his jeans were already becoming, he guided the horse up the hill behind the house. He, Chloe and Owen all had their favorite parts of the ranch, but he'd never told anyone where his was, a little knoll that afforded a great view to the west, what he considered the most perfect place in the world to watch a sunset. So as the sun slid toward the horizon, that's where he pointed the horse.

They didn't talk for several minutes, but he thought he could detect Natalie relaxing. Not wanting to cause her to tense up again, he kept silent—at least outwardly. In his head, things resembled the spin cycle of the washing machine. Despite the fact that he and Natalie hadn't really spent that much time together, he knew little of her life in Kansas, and his instincts told him that her thoughts were sometimes a million miles away, he still felt drawn to her in a way he didn't understand. In the safety of his own head, he imagined riding around the ranch with her like this for years to come. Maybe that was crazy, but he couldn't seem to help it.

They didn't really know each other, but his gut told him they were well matched. Though he loved Linnea like a sister, she was a city girl still learning the ways of ranch life. But Natalie? She wouldn't shy away from cattle and horses, from getting dirty and sweaty when the job required it.

And damned if that thought didn't lead to others of even more reasons for getting sweaty. He tried to resettle himself, but Natalie must have realized why because she stiffened.

Damn.

"How's your leg doing?" he asked, trying to deflect attention away from what was going on behind his fly.

"Okay." She didn't sound particularly convincing, and he considered turning the horse around.

But they were almost to the spot he wanted to show her, and from the look of the sky toward the west, it was going to be a stunning sunset. A couple more undulations in the landscape and they arrived. Natalie's little intake of breath made him smile.

"It's beautiful," she said.

Those two simple words, spoken with such appreciation for a view some people would consider barren, lifted his heart. And damn if he didn't think he could fall for this woman.

"Yeah, feels like you can really think and breathe here."

"As if the rest of the world and its problems have fallen away."

Their awkward moment seemingly forgotten, she watched as the sun headed toward the other side of the world. He glanced at the sunset a few times, but his gaze kept drifting back to her. He didn't think she realized how much she'd relaxed against the arm he had at her back, making sure she stayed safely atop the horse.

"It'd be nice if everything in life was this simple, wouldn't it?" she asked when the sun was nearly gone from sight.

"Yeah." Unable to stop himself, he reached up and smoothed a few tendrils of her hair away from her face.

He expected her to tense up again. Instead, she slowly turned her head to face him. Taking that and the open look in her eyes as permission, he lifted her chin gently, allowing her time to pull away if that's what she wanted. But when she didn't retreat, he lowered his lips to hers.

GARRETT'S LIPS FELT like heaven, so much better than Natalie had imagined. Some rational part of her brain told her this was wrong, that she should pull away, protect herself and him. But she shoved that voice of reason away, wanting this moment of bliss to last forever.

When Garrett deepened the kiss, she allowed

herself to be swept up in the feel of his arms around her, his warmth, his strength, the taste of coffee that had gotten him through his long day of work. His arms pulled her closer, and he uttered a moan that sent pure desire racing along her veins. Her body leaned into his of its own accord.

Pain caused her to gasp and jerk away from him. The haze of desire scrambled her brain cells, so it took a moment for her to connect the feeling of pain to the fact that she'd mashed her injured arm against his belt buckle.

"You okay?" Garrett asked, the genuine concern in his voice making her thundering heart expand.

"Yeah, I'll live." But reality started rushing back into her brain with such force that it nearly knocked her to the ground. He'd kissed her, and she'd kissed him back. The enormity of that mistake hurt more than the pain in her arm. "But I think I could use one of my pain pills."

If only they worked on a heart full of different shades of sorrow.

She glanced up at him in time to see a flicker of doubt, but he tugged on the reins, guiding the horse back toward the main part of the ranch. The tension returned to her muscles as she waited for him to say something. But he didn't, and she wasn't sure if she was glad for that or not.

Garrett was just as careful helping her dismount when they returned to the barn as he'd been when he aided her in mounting, but the awkwardness between them had grown with each clop of the horse's hooves on the way back.

"Thanks for the ride," she said when she was safely on the ground with her crutches again.

He finally met her gaze. "Hope you enjoyed it."

"I did." Though she knew she should walk away, she didn't want to. "You were right. I've been going a little nuts with nothing to do." And with her father's confession eating big, gaping holes in her conscience.

"Maybe you'll heal soon and things can get back to normal."

No doubt about it. Garrett definitely suspected something other than her injuries had come between them up on that hillside. But maybe the distance he was putting between them, both physically and emotionally, was a good thing.

With her heart heavy, she gave him a quick nod and made her way out of the barn and toward the house when part of her wanted to keep going down the driveway and flag down the first driver who came by on the road.

When she reached the back door, Wayne was there to greet her with a big smile on his weathered face. "How was your ride?"

Did he look a little too hopeful? But for what?

Was he hoping she and Garrett would get together? The memory of their kiss sent warmth rushing through her body along with the desire for so much more. But it was not to be, and the first opportunity she had to get off this ranch, she was taking it.

"Um, good. But I might have overdone it. I think I'm going to turn in early."

"But dinner's almost ready."

Somehow she managed to not allow her stomach to grumble at the smell of good Texas chili. "Maybe I'll eat some later. You and Garrett go ahead without me."

She hated herself for causing the momentary look of disappointment on Wayne's face. He'd once been like a second father to her, sometimes more of one than her own, and she ached to hug him. Instead, she offered a small smile.

"Okay, you rest. There will be plenty left, so you just let me know when you get hungry."

She nodded, but as shaky as she felt at the moment, she knew she wasn't going to come out of her room that night, at least not until Garrett and his dad were sound asleep.

But once she was closed up in Chloe's old room, she felt even more trapped. She ignored her growing hunger as she listened to the Brody men go about their evening rituals. She didn't even turn on a light, not wanting to invite a knock on her door. Instead, she lay in the bed and listened to their muted voices, the scrape of their boots on the floor, the singing of the water pipes as someone took a shower.

She imagined it was Garrett with warm water and soap rushing over his skin, then imagined herself stepping under the flow of water with him, letting him kiss her again as he had earlier. She'd had the momentary thought that if she indulged in just one kiss, she'd be able to survive on that memory. But it wasn't true. Now that she knew what it felt like to be held in Garrett's arms, to feel passion rising between them, she didn't want to let it go. But she didn't have a choice. She couldn't stay and not tell him the truth. But if she shared the real reason for her return to Blue Falls, she would not only hurt him but also his entire family. And what were the chances that he'd ever look at her the same way again?

She squeezed her eyes against sudden tears and wished she'd never returned to Blue Falls. Nothing good could come of it.

Chapter Ten

Natalie stared out the window the next morning as she wondered if any of the taxi services in Austin would drive out to Blue Falls to pick her up. After what had happened between her and Garrett the day before, there was no way she could stay under his roof any longer.

Someone knocked on the door. She'd already ignored one knock earlier, pretending to still be asleep. But she couldn't keep doing that without sending up even more red flags than she was currently waving.

"Come in," she said as she pushed herself to her feet with the aid of her crutches.

Instead of a tentative poking in of the head, however, the door flew open to reveal a woman about her own age.

"Oh, my God, it's true! You're really here."

Natalie stood dumbstruck at the vision before her, a younger version of Karen Brody. "Chloe?"

"Yes!" Chloe rushed forward and wrapped Natalie in her arms. "I'm so happy to see you."

Natalie had to press her eyes closed to keep a fresh batch of tears from flowing as a result of the twisted mess of happiness, sorrow, regret and countless other emotions inside her. It felt so good to be held by her childhood best friend again that she found herself hugging Chloe back, hanging on as if her friend was a life preserver in the midst of a wide, tumultuous sea doing its best to drown her.

Chloe stepped back but kept her hands planted on Natalie's shoulders. "Why didn't you tell me you were coming back to Blue Falls? I just can't believe it. I have so many questions for you."

Natalie smiled despite the maelstrom inside her head. Chloe was just how she remembered her, full of life. At least how she remembered her before her mother had been killed. Natalie fought to keep her smile in place in the wake of that memory.

"It was sort of a spur-of-the-moment trip."

"I didn't think I'd ever see you again when I never heard from you."

Natalie opened her mouth to ask what Chloe meant when her friend had been the one not to write back. But before she made the mistake of speaking, Natalie realized what must have happened. A hot surge of anger toward her parents made her stumble.

"Sorry. I shouldn't make you stand there like that," Chloe said. "Come into the kitchen and have some breakfast. We've got a lot of catching up to do."

The distance from the bedroom to the kitchen wasn't far, but Natalie was thankful for the time it gave her to try to calm herself, to set aside for now the anger at the realization that her parents hadn't ever sent her letters to Chloe. And that her mother hadn't thought to tell her that before she'd come on this disaster of a trip.

She forced herself to take a couple of slow breaths during which she reminded herself that her mom's mind had probably been far away from those letters in recent days.

Chloe pulled out a chair for Natalie and nodded to it as she went to scoop up some pancakes. She warmed them up in the microwave for a few seconds then did the same with some maple syrup, before setting it all in front of Natalie with a fresh cup of coffee. It was so like something her mother would have done that it carved out another piece of Natalie's heart.

As she looked across the table to where her friend sat with her own cup of coffee, Natalie realized that here was another opportunity to finally tell the truth. But Chloe absolutely glowed with happiness. So Natalie shoved the past down deeper and allowed herself to be carried on the waves of conversation that came so naturally it was wonderful and painful at the same time. They talked about Chloe's new husband, Owen's new wife, their careers, how Natalie had helped Penelope after her injury, basically anything and everything that didn't have to do with the night Natalie's father ended Chloe's mother's life.

When the morning gave way to afternoon, Chloe made them grilled ham and cheese sandwiches and they kept talking.

"Shouldn't you be at work or with your new husband?" Natalie finally asked.

Chloe waved away Natalie's concern. "I don't go back to work until tomorrow, and I've been with Wyatt nonstop for a week."

Natalie laughed. "Already tired of him?"

Color rose in Chloe's cheeks. "Not at all. I can't imagine ever getting tired of Wyatt."

The obvious love in Chloe's words transported Natalie back to those moments in Garrett's arms, to how much she wished it could have gone on forever.

"What about you?" Chloe asked, jerking Natalie back to the present. "Anyone special in your life?"

"Um, no."

"Well, that didn't sound convincing."

"There's no one."

"Well, stick around here long enough and we'll cure that."

Natalie's gaze shot to Chloe's. "What?"

Chloe laughed and reached across the table to squeeze Natalie's hand. "Don't look so scared. It's just common knowledge that if you slow down too long in Blue Falls, Verona Charles will match you up with someone. She's our very own Cupid."

"Oh, I've heard about her, but I won't be here that long. In fact, as soon as I can, I need to get back home and return to work." Though giving vaccinations to cattle and helping birth foals was going to be interesting in her current condition.

"Well, until then I plan to enjoy every minute I can with you."

Part of Natalie loved that idea, but another very nervous part didn't know how long she could handle it.

"In fact, you're coming with us to the local rodeo tonight."

"Probably not the best idea with me knocking around on crutches."

"Nonsense. I hear you've been making your way around the ranch, even went on a ride yesterday. Did you get two words out of Garrett? He's still the quietest of the three of us."

"A few." And one kiss that scorched her all the way down to the tips of her toes. "Really, though, I'll be fine here by myself. You all go on and have fun."

"You do realize you won't win an argument with me, right? Besides, the proceeds go to the local animal shelter, and I know you won't be able to say no to that."

Natalie relented, mainly so that she didn't seem too determined not to go. And despite her job, she hadn't been to a rodeo in a long time. Might be fun if she could manage to push aside all the guilt gnawing at her.

Thankfully, Natalie was able to ride to the

rodeo with Chloe and Wyatt, who greeted Natalie with a big ole kiss on the cheek as if he'd known her all her life.

"Careful or you'll make me jealous," Chloe said with a playful punch to Wyatt's shoulder.

Natalie leaned her crutches out a little and nodded toward her cast. "Yes, because I'm such a catch."

"I've only got eyes for you," Wyatt said and then leaned Chloe back and laid the kind of kiss on her that women dreamed about.

A kiss that had Natalie averting her gaze, which landed on Garrett. He was looking straight at her, at least until she made eye contact.

"Um, sorry about that," Chloe said when Wyatt righted her. "My husband seems to think we're still on our honeymoon."

Natalie shifted her gaze away from where Garrett was getting into his truck with his dad.

"No need to apologize. You technically still are on your honeymoon."

"See?" Wyatt said. "Natalie understands."

Natalie couldn't help but laugh, happy that her friend had found someone so wonderful. Even so, she felt like a third wheel as they rode into Blue Falls. She knew they weren't trying to exclude her, but she supposed you couldn't help it when you were in love. Her thoughts drifted to Garrett again, and she wondered if they could get to that point if things were different.

When they reached the rodeo grounds, she said she wanted to stretch her legs and that she'd meet them at the grandstand before the rodeo got under way. She wandered through the rows of vendors and ended up where the local animal shelter had set up an area filled with animals available for adoption. Her heart went out to each of the animals, and it wasn't the first time she wished she could adopt them all.

A friendly yip drew her attention to a little sheltie looking up at her with the friendliest expression she'd ever seen on a pup's face. "Aw, hey there, sweetie." She made her way over to where he stood wagging his tail. "Aren't you a handsome little guy?"

She started to lean over to pet him, but a sharp pain traveled the length of her leg, causing her to curse under her breath.

"Let me." The rumble of Garrett's voice registered as he leaned past her to pick up the puppy.

As soon as Garrett turned to face her with the dog held in his arms, the puppy wiggled in excitement and licked her chin.

Garrett laughed. "I think he likes you."

Trying to ignore the fact that Garrett was so close she could smell his woodsy male scent, she brought her face down level with the puppy's. He wriggled his way out of Garrett's arms into hers. When she teetered a bit, Garrett moved quickly to steady her with his warm hand at the small of her back. She looked up into his eyes, and her breath caught.

"Maybe you should take him."

That's exactly what she wanted to do as visions of making love to Garrett filled her head. Wait, no, that wasn't what he meant. She broke eye contact and leaned her cheek against the soft fur atop the pup's head.

"I'd be sorely tempted if I were home," she said. For some reason, she felt an instant attachment to the animal, much the same as she had with Garrett. Neither made any sense.

"You can bring him out to the ranch. It'd actually do Roscoe and Cletus some good to have a younger pup around for a while."

"I don't know."

As if the pup could understand, he whimpered and licked her cheek with a renewed burst of enthusiasm.

"See, he loves you already."

Just hearing the word *love* on Garrett's lips made her insides flutter.

"He's such a lovable little guy," one of the volunteers manning the adoption area said, drawing Natalie's attention. "He's come close to being adopted a few times, but it's always fallen through."

Natalie imagined his little puppy heart getting his hopes for a home up only to be shattered repeatedly. And she couldn't do it to him again. She met Garrett's gaze.

"Are you sure it's okay for me to—"

"Yes," he said before she even had a chance to finish.

A few minutes later, she was the happy owner of a new little sheltie that seemed thrilled to be out of the pen and on a leash.

"I don't know what I was thinking," she said as she watched the puppy jump around Garrett's feet as if he'd just been sprung from prison. "I can barely take care of myself."

"You seem to be doing pretty well to me."

Oh, how wrong he was, but she kept that thought to herself.

As they reached the grandstand, she found that the Brody clan had staked out their claim to the first several spots on the first two rows so she wouldn't have to climb the stairs.

"Hey there," a handsome young guy who had to be Owen said as he got to his feet. "Long time, no see."

"Yeah." She glanced from him to the lovely redhead who must be Linnea. "Congrats on your wedding."

After introductions, Chloe noticed the pup in Garrett's arms. "You seem to have picked up a passenger."

Natalie caught the too-curious look her friend gave her then Garrett. Oh no, she couldn't let

Chloe or anyone else get any ideas about her and Garrett. Despite their kiss, that was a dead-end street.

"I seem to have lost my mind and just adopted a puppy," she said then shifted her eyes to Wayne. "I hope you don't mind. We'll both be out of your hair soon."

"Heck no. Will do those old hounds some good to have this little guy to harass them."

She laughed a little. "That's what Garrett said." She glanced over her shoulder before she thought about what she was doing, and her heart sank at the way Garrett's expression had dimmed for some reason.

Though he sat beside her during the rodeo and seemed to have a good time, she couldn't shake the feeling that something was bothering him.

Chloe leaned close to her. "Something wrong?"

"No. Well, nothing other than the fact that my leg is itching under this cast."

Even though it was true, at least partially, Natalie wasn't sure Chloe believed her.

"Don't stick anything under the cast to scratch the skin," Chloe said, shifting into doctor mode. "You could irritate the skin and get it infected. Use a hair dryer on its low, cool setting, and blow air down between the cast and your leg."

"Wouldn't have thought of that. Thanks."

"Is she showing off her fancy medical degree again?" Owen asked from behind Chloe.

"I seem to remember that fancy medical degree keeping you from being sick on a certain ship recently."

"Oh, fine, throw that in my face."

Everyone laughed, and the pup wiggled in Natalie's lap.

"So what are you going to call this little guy?" Owen asked.

"I don't know." She glanced at Garrett, trying to act casual. "What do you think? You're the one who convinced me to adopt him."

"Bruiser?"

The pup sneezed and shook his head, causing several chuckles.

"I think your suggestion just got vetoed," Wyatt said.

As Natalie looked into the puppy's eyes, a name drifted into her mind seemingly from out of nowhere. "Milo." It fit so perfectly, as if the dog had been born to it.

Garrett scratched the pup between his ears. "Milo, it is."

As Natalie watched the bull-riding event, gasping each time a rider got thrown, Garrett shifted next to her. The moment his thigh touched hers, she stiffened. Trying to distract herself, she turned to say something, anything, to Chloe. But her friend was speaking to Linnea and a couple of their friends who'd come over from a different part of the grandstand. Something about the way they all had their heads bent together clanged the suspicion bell in Natalie's head, but she didn't feel comfortable enough to ask what they were talking about. So she was stuck with trying to focus on the rest of the bull riding instead of the warmth seeping from Garrett's leg into hers.

When the rodeo was over, Wayne scooped up Milo. "How about you and I get out of here, little man?"

"There's room with us," Natalie said.

Chloe wrapped her arm around Natalie's. "But our night isn't over."

"It's not?"

"Nope. There's another fund-raiser for the shelter at the music hall."

Though Natalie was tired, she actually liked the idea of going somewhere crowded. The less time she had to spend alone with the Brodys, the better. In fact, it was high time she found another way to get home. Maybe she could get one of her coworkers to fly down to Texas and drive back with her, though she didn't relish eating the cost of a last-minute plane ticket or hours alone in the car with someone she normally saw only at work.

Natalie changed her mind about spending time at the music hall, however, when they arrived and she saw that the event planned was a bachelor auction. The last thing she needed to think about was the only bachelor in the place whom she had the slightest interest in.

"This is going to be fun," Chloe said as she stepped up beside Natalie.

She eyed Chloe and Linnea, then their friends Keri, Elissa and India. "Correct me if I'm wrong, but aren't all of you married already?"

"Yes, but you're not." Chloe waggled her eyebrows.

"I remember Owen being the mischievous one in the family."

Chloe shrugged. "What can I say? He and Wyatt have rubbed off on me."

The next thing she knew, Natalie was being ushered toward a table at the side of the room adjacent to the dance floor. Several couples twirled and boot-scooted around to the sound of a Big & Rich song.

"I can't believe I let you talk me into this."

Natalie turned at the sound of Garrett's voice. He stood on the other side of the table talking to Chloe and Linnea.

"Hush, it's for a good cause," Chloe said. "And it's one date."

"Yeah, what could go wrong?" The sarcasm dripped off his words like thick syrup.

Natalie was pretty sure her heart had missed a

few beats at the realization that one of the bachelors up for auction was the man she'd kissed and very much wanted to kiss again. Were it not for the secret she still harbored, she'd be hard-pressed not to empty her bank account bidding on him. And yes, she realized that was at least partially because she hated the idea of someone else buying a date with him, someone else he might kiss since she'd pulled away and done her best to avoid him since.

Ugh. She resisted the need to bang her head on the table.

"Welcome, everyone!"

Natalie shifted her gaze to the stage, where a woman she'd seen earlier at the pet-adoption area of the fairgrounds had stepped up to the microphone.

"We're glad to have you all here tonight to help us raise some much-needed funds to keep doing the work we do at the animal shelter.

Thanks for coming out to the rodeo and to our first-ever bachelor auction!"

That drew a round of whistles and applause from the ladies in the crowd.

"Now, if you aren't in the market for a date with a hunky bachelor, we've also got some tables set up in the back with several silent auction items."

If Natalie could walk without crutches, she'd head straight for the silent auction. No, she'd hoof it to where her car was still parked at the Country Vista Inn and race toward the interstate as if the devil himself was chasing her. She did not trust herself to hide her feelings whenever someone in the crowd made the winning bid for Garrett.

"You ready?" Chloe asked as she sank into the chair next to Natalie.

"Should be amusing, I guess."

"Lots of good choices."

Natalie met Chloe's gaze. "I'm not bidding. There's no sense in going out with someone here when I'll be going home soon." And probably never stepping foot in Blue Falls again.

"As I told Garrett, it's just one date. What could it hurt?"

Oh, it could hurt. It could hurt a lot.

With that lovely thought, Natalie shifted her attention to the stage, where a handsome guy named Pablo was first up. He looked as uncomfortable as Natalie imagined she'd be in the same situation.

Natalie tried her best not to look at where Garrett now stood in line on the opposite side of the stage, but it was impossible. She might glance at the middle-aged banker or the young sheriff's deputy, but her gaze refused to stay on the stage. Only when Greg Bozeman hopped up on stage and started working the crowd did she relax a little and laugh along with everyone else.

"He hasn't changed a bit since we were kids," she said.

"Nope. Remind me to tell you the mooning-on-the-water-tower story."

"That should be good."

After Greg urged up the bidding on his date and the winner squealed in delight, Natalie squirmed in her seat. Garrett was up next, and she couldn't pull her eyes away from him as his long legs brought him up onto the stage.

"Ladies, next up is Garrett Brody. At the rate the Brody siblings are getting married lately, this might be your only chance."

More laughter filled the room, but this time Natalie didn't join in. At the moment, she'd give anything to be anywhere else.

"Can I get an opening bid?"

Someone across the room yelled out, "Fifty!"

Natalie tried to keep her gaze from drifting to the stage, but again it was impossible. When she realized Garrett was looking at her, it was like a shock wave traveling along her veins.

"Four hundred!"

Natalie jerked her attention to Chloe. "Did you just bid on your brother?"

"I'm what you'd call a designated bidder."

A glance back at the stage showed that Garrett was every bit as confused as her.

Also looking surprised, the lady from the shelter said, "Hey, if you're willing to bid to keep your brother from going on a date, we'll still take your money."

More laughter echoed through the room, but unease began to build in the pit of Natalie's stomach.

"Anybody want to top four hundred dollars?"

When nobody responded and the bidding ended, cheering erupted from every other woman at Natalie's table. Chloe leaned her shoulder against Natalie's.

"You can thank me later."

"What?" The truth of what Chloe, Linnea and their friends had done, what the whispered conversation had been about earlier, hit Natalie. "You didn't."

"We did."

"Why would you do that?"

"Because it's obvious you two like each other."

"God, Chloe, this was a really bad idea." Panic welled inside Natalie like the storm surge coming off a hurricane.

Chloe grabbed Natalie's hand and squeezed. "Just go and have some fun."

"I don't even live here." Why couldn't anyone understand that?

Because from their point of view, she'd made no move to leave.

Because deep down, a part of her did want to live here with these people, with Garrett.

"So, care to tell me what's going on?" Garrett asked as he walked up in front of his sister.

"You're going on a date with Natalie."

Up on the stage, the auction came to an end and the band began to play, drawing people back to the dance floor—including everyone at Natalie's table but her.

Left with Garrett looming over her, she slowly lifted her gaze to his. "I swear I didn't know what they were up to."

He lowered himself to the chair Chloe had vacated. "I know my sister well enough to believe you."

"You don't have to go through with it."

"It's no problem."

Not exactly bowled over by his enthusiasm, she thought maybe she could leave town before the date that had been foisted upon them.

"How about a trip to the drive-in tomorrow night? They just opened one up this summer between here and Fredericksburg."

She frantically searched for a plausible excuse but came up empty.

"Um, sure." So much for avoidance.

Chapter Eleven

As Garrett pulled into the drive-in the next
night, he feared this date was going to end up
as bad as some of his others. Natalie had been
quiet during the entire ride, and he couldn't help
but wonder if it was because she was nervous or
just wishing the whole thing was over. Maybe
she simply knew that it didn't make any sense,
just as their kiss hadn't. After all, she'd said
herself the night before that she'd be gone soon.
Of course he'd known that when he kissed her,
but in that moment he'd not been able to keep
himself from capturing her lips, from finding
out if they tasted as sweet as they looked.

They had.

And despite the fact that they hadn't had a repeat or even spoken the first word about it, he couldn't help the building attraction he felt toward her. Seeing her face light up as she played with Milo was just about the prettiest thing he'd ever seen. Some gut instinct told him that she hadn't had a lot to smile about lately, so if he got her to smile once tonight he was going to call the date a success.

After paying for their tickets, he drove up to the back row and parked. "Want some popcorn?"

"Sure. That sounds nice."

She barely made eye contact, as if she was afraid to hold his gaze for too long.

He made his way to the concession stand for the popcorn and drinks, but then an idea popped into his head, something that might put a smile on Natalie's face and ease the tension between them.

When he returned to the truck and opened the door, Natalie glanced over at him and her eyes widened.

"Did we pick up a basketball team on the way that I missed?"

"I didn't know what all you liked, so I just got a little of everything."

He set the tray of junk food between their seats.

"We are going to get sick from all this," she said with a shake of her head.

"Oh well, we'll just both moan with belly-aches. Everyone nearby will think we're having a great time."

Her eyes widened even more as she looked up at him, and then she burst out laughing.

Yeah, the money he'd just dropped on everything from hot dogs to nachos to candy bars was worth every penny.

They munched away as the movie started. He glanced across the truck at her a few times and was happy the movie playing was a comedy that made her laugh.

About halfway through, she reached for another Milk Dud then dropped the nearly empty box back onto the cardboard tray. "Ugh, none of this even looks good now. I feel the need to immediately go join a gym. Or start a cross-country run like Forrest Gump."

Feeling the same way, Garrett grabbed the remains of their snack-a-thon and stepped out of the truck. After dumping everything into the nearest trash can, he came back to find Natalie watching him.

"Thanks for this," she said. "You didn't have to go through with the blindsided date, but it's been fun."

"Yeah." He reached over and ran his thumb across her cheek. "Got to say this is one of the nicer things that's caught me by surprise."

He saw hesitation in her eyes.

"Garrett—"

"Let's just enjoy the night." He could have kissed her then, but something told him to wait even though he was afraid she'd pull away again. He'd swear he could see a war going on behind her gaze. When she leaned into his touch on her cheek, his heart hammered in his chest and he captured her mouth with his.

His entire body wanted to touch her, so he pulled her close and deepened the kiss. After some initial hesitance, Natalie relaxed and met him halfway. His heart thundered in his ears, and his arousal strained against the inside of his jeans. He hadn't wanted a woman so much in a long time. Ever.

Damn, he wished they were somewhere alone,

where no one would interrupt them, where they had the whole night stretched out in front of them.

Gradually, the sound of engines starting dragged him out of his lust-drugged haze. He glanced out the windshield toward the field full of taillights then back to Natalie.

"Looks like the movie is over."

"Oh?"

Did she sound as if she thought that was bad news?

"I don't want the date to end now. Do you?"

She stared up at him so long that he was afraid of her answer. But then she shook her head, and he moved to start the truck's engine. Natalie allowed him to hold her hand as he drove back toward Blue Falls, but before he got there he took a road that led to a spot overlooking the lake.

"Just past those trees has a nice view," he said.

"Okay."

He hopped out of the truck, grabbing a blanket for them to sit on before wrapping his arms around her shoulder and behind her knees then carrying her up the darkened path.

"Garrett, carrying me to the porch is one thing, but up a trail?"

"It's not far."

Still, when they reached their destination, his breath was coming a little heavier. Granted, some of that might be because he had Natalie pressed close to him. As he reluctantly set her on her feet, he kept a firm hold on her so she wouldn't stumble.

"It's so pretty," she said as she looked out across the lake toward the lights of downtown Blue Falls.

The *Lady Fleur* paddle wheeler was out for an evening cruise as well, the string of white lights surrounding its deck reflecting off the water.

"Stay there," he said as he spread out the blanket. "Don't want you falling down the hillside and breaking your other leg."

"Not high on my list, either."

When he had the blanket spread on the ground, he helped her sit then sat close to her.

"This is nice, so peaceful," she said, sounding like someone who'd been searching for peace for a long time.

He thought about asking her what had been bothering her, but honestly, he just wanted to hold her again, push reality and responsibility away for one night.

"So, any interest in kissing your date?"

She hesitated a moment before looking up at him. "Maybe."

He grinned and framed her face with his hands.

NATALIE KNEW SHE should end what was happening between her and Garrett, shouldn't have even gone on the date with him, but she couldn't seem to help herself. How much will-power was she expected to have anyway when the guy she could so easily fall for wanted to hold her in his arms and kiss her?

It was just one night. If she could guard her heart, guard the secret that might make him hate her, maybe she could allow herself this one night. The feel of his mouth on hers was more intoxicating than any drink could ever be. She'd have to go home soon or risk becoming addicted.

Garrett's hands made their way underneath the back of her shirt and moved slowly up her spine until they encountered her bra clasp. On a quick intake of breath, he released it. With every caress, every kiss, every extra-fast heart-beat, a part of Natalie screamed at her to stop, to either tell Garrett the truth or leave him behind for good. But that part of her was overwhelmed by the delicious sensations he was sending through her body.

She ran her fingers through his close-cropped hair as his mouth traveled from hers down to her neck. As he eased her back onto the blanket with one of his hands behind her head to protect it, she realized just how much she wanted him.

Garrett held her gaze as he slowly shoved her shirt up and over her breasts, baring them to him. "Is this too much?"

She heard in his voice how much he hoped she didn't stop him, and in that moment she knew she couldn't despite all the reasons she should. She'd lost so much lately, and all those years ago, that she couldn't deny herself or him.

"No." But as he lowered his mouth to her breast and unzipped her shorts, she grabbed his shoulders and stopped him. "What if someone comes up here?"

"They won't."

And she believed him that he would protect this time they had together.

Though her cast made undressing a bit of an extra challenge, Garrett took his time with her and didn't appear to become frustrated. She couldn't believe she was doing this, stripping down to nothing underneath the stars. But with each movement, her desire for Garrett grew. She lifted her hands to his shirt and started un-buttoning it. When she spread the shirt wide, her breath caught. Even in the dim light cast by the stars and a sliver of moon, he was magnifi-cent. Unable to stop herself, she ran her hands up and over his chest. Garrett's sharp inhale revved her up even more, and she grabbed the open halves of his shirt and pulled him down for a kiss.

The moment his bare chest touched hers, she moaned into his mouth.

He lifted his head to look down at her, to run

the pad of his finger across her wet lips. "I want to make love to you, Natalie. I have ever since that first kiss, probably before."

Even with lust and quite possibly love rushing through her body, she still took a moment to look deeply into his eyes. This wasn't just a man looking to get laid. More was going on here, and that should have scared her away. But it didn't. It only made her want him more.

She couldn't find the words to tell him how she felt. Instead, she lifted her head and kissed him deeply, giving him silent permission to keep going.

He rolled away to remove his clothes, and her heart beat at a frantic pace when he appeared above her and gently spread her legs.

"I don't want to hurt you."

"You won't."

He kissed her again as his hands slid under her hips. She felt herself grow wet as he lifted her at an angle and slid inside her.

She gasped as he filled her.

"Are you okay?"

She smiled up at him. "Yes." She ran her fingertips down the middle of his chest then lower, causing him to tense. "Better than okay."

Natalie ceased to care if anyone was nearby or what daylight would bring. In this glorious moment, she was going to enjoy all the erotic sensations sparking from her brain to every nerve ending.

Garrett evidently felt the same because his restraint seemed to flee as he began to move quicker. She silently cursed her cast because she wanted to wrap her legs around him, allowing him to go even deeper.

As if he could read her desire, he shifted so that he filled her even more, increasing the pace with each stroke. The muscles inside her began to tense, and each of Garrett's movements brought her closer to completion. By the sound of his ragged breaths beside her ear, he was in a similar state.

"Faster." She hadn't meant to say it out loud, but it was what she wanted, and Garrett complied until she stiffened and came apart. His release followed quickly on the heels of hers, and his moan of absolute pleasure made her smile and feel like the most powerful woman in the world.

After their breathing slowed, Garrett pulled her close and kissed her with such tenderness that it brought home the truth. She loved him. The realization nearly brought tears to her eyes, and part of her wondered if there was some way to make this work. But how could he ever hold her like this again knowing that her father had killed his mother? Even if he didn't blame her, that horrible thought would always be there.

"You okay?" he asked. "I didn't hurt you, did I?"

"I'm fine." She caressed his strong jaw and felt a soul-deep yearning for a life with this man. It was on her lips to tell him that she loved him, but that wasn't fair, not when she was lying to him by omission.

Tomorrow she would deal with the aftermath of what had just happened between them, but for now all she wanted was to be held in Garrett's arms for as long as possible.

WHEN THEY RETURNED to the ranch, Garrett didn't want to go inside. He feared that when night gave way to day, Natalie would pretend it hadn't happened as she had after their first kiss. And as crazy as it sounded, he didn't think he could live through that. No matter that they had spent only a few days together after two decades of not laying eyes on each other, he was having thoughts as if Natalie might be the one.

How that was going to work, he had no idea.

All he knew was that he couldn't go another moment without kissing her again. So as soon as he carried her up the front porch steps, he pulled her into his arms and kissed her until he was forced to come up to breathe.

"Be careful," she said with a small laugh. "You're going to scar poor Roscoe and Cletus."

He glanced over his shoulder to where the dogs didn't seem at all interested in the nearby humans. "I guarantee you that is not the first kiss they've seen on this porch."

"That right?"

"Yeah, you seem to forget the newest family members spent a good bit of recovery time here, as well. I think we're going to have to get a B and B license."

"I don't think what happened tonight is typically on the menu at a B and B."

"That was a special deal."

"Oh, how much is that going to cost me?"

"Another kiss."

He lost track of the minutes as they stood on the porch kissing, but he caught a small wince on her face that told him she was ready to rest her leg. He nodded toward the door.

"Time for some sleep."

She yawned. "I think you're right."

He held the door for her. "You go on. I'm going to check on the animals before I turn in."

"Okay, good night."

He stole one final kiss. "Good night. Sweet dreams."

The way she smiled at him made him think that she was hoping her dreams would be of him.

After she disappeared into the house, he strode out to the fence that ran from beside the barn down the length of the driveway. He leaned on the fence and looked up at the blanket of stars above, thought about the meteor shower they'd watched together. If he saw a shooting star tonight, he knew exactly what he would wish for—a miracle that would keep Natalie Todd in his life.

NATALIE AWOKE SLOWLY, trying to hang on to the dream in which she and Garrett were wrapped around each other in an embrace that filled her with more love than she thought possible. As dreams were wont to do, however, the image faded as she woke to find the sun streaming in the window.

As if that bright light was illuminating every nook and cranny of her soul, the bliss of the dream was replaced by a heart in turmoil. Her evening with Garrett had been the best night of her life, and she knew she would hold it close forever. But now that the star-studded sky wasn't winking down at them, filling her head with romantic thoughts, she knew she shouldn't have let it go so far—at least not without telling him the truth first.

As she lay there staring at the ceiling, she realized that all the times she'd told herself it would be better for her to just leave and take her secret with her had been nothing more than fear talking. Fear that Chloe and her family would hate her. Fear that she wouldn't be able to get through the telling without falling apart. Fear that the feelings that had started growing for Garrett the moment he stole that first cheese fry would be thrown back in her face.

And now she'd made love to him, fallen in love with the grown-up version of that boy who'd captured her heart so long ago. Telling him was going to be so much worse, but she couldn't avoid it any longer. If it had been her mother killed by some unknown driver, she'd want to know the truth. Though she'd maintained the need to tell the entire family at once, things had changed. Because of what they'd shared and how she felt about him, she had to tell Garrett first.

The nausea that had accompanied her to Blue Falls returned, so she made her way to the bathroom and splashed cold water on her face. After fumbling her way through getting ready, she headed up the hallway. If Garrett was keeping to his typical schedule, he should be in the barn. She only hoped he was alone. Just thinking about Wayne, Owen or any of the other Brodys there as well made her heart ache. How had she ever thought she could sit across from all of them and tell them what her father had asked her to? The weight of all those stares at once, all the anger and sorrow, would be too much to bear.

When she reached the living room, instead of heading immediately to the kitchen door, she detoured to the pictures along the mantel. She lifted a family photo from about a year before Karen had died. All those smiles looking back at Natalie made what she was about to do even worse.

She placed the framed photograph back in its spot and took a deep, shaky breath. Knowing it wasn't going to get any easier if she waited longer and not wanting to risk Garrett leaving before she could talk to him, she started her trek to the barn. Her hands shook so much that it was difficult to keep a firm grip on her crutches, and by the time she reached the entrance to the barn she felt as if she was going to be sick or pass out, or quite possibly both. She stopped and forced herself to take slow, even breaths.

When she finally stepped into the barn, it took a few moments for her eyes to adjust to the dimmer light. But then she saw Garrett and she wanted nothing more than to be held in his arms again. He caught sight of her and headed toward her.

"Good morning," he said as he came close. The look in his eyes said he was going to kiss her. If she let him, she feared she'd lose her resolve to tell him the truth. So she took a couple of awkward steps away, causing Garrett to stop in his tracks and give her a confused look.

"You okay?"

"Yeah." She paused and glanced down at the ground before forcing herself to meet his gaze. "Actually, no. I need to tell you something."

He sighed. "You regret last night."

"No, I don't. I had a wonderful time." It had been so far beyond wonderful, but how could she convey that with mere words? "It's just that…I should have told you something before anything happened between us."

Garrett crossed his arms and took what appeared to be an unconscious step backward. "Okay."

She began to shake so much that she made her way to a stack of hay bales and leaned back against them. "I didn't just come to Blue Falls for old time's sake. I made a promise to my dad the night he died that I'd come back here and… give your family a message."

The lines on Garrett's forehead deepened. "Your dad?"

She bit her lip and wished with all her heart there was an easier way to say this. "He…" Her voice broke, and she took a moment to swallow past a lump in her throat that felt as if it were the size of a softball. "He was the one who hit your mom's car that night."

For what felt like forever, Garrett just stared at her, as if he couldn't have possibly heard her correctly.

"What night?"

He knew what she meant. She could see it in his eyes. But she knew in her heart that he was hoping what he was hearing wasn't true, the same as she had the night her father had told her.

"He'd been drinking, and he hit her car. He said that he checked on her, but when he saw…" Again, her voice broke, and this time it was accompanied by tears welling in her eyes. "I'm so sorry, Garrett, but he ran. And he dragged us all away from here in fear."

Garrett stared at her hard with a look so piercing she'd swear she could feel the heat of it on her skin. "Your father was drunk when he hit my mom? And then he ran away?"

She nodded.

"The bastard ran away and left us with nothing but horrible questions." His face transformed with the darkest look of hatred she'd ever seen. "You've known all this time and said nothing?"

"I fully intended to tell your family the night I arrived, but Owen had just gotten married. He, Chloe and their spouses were headed out on their honeymoon trip. It…it just didn't feel right to bring such awful news into such a happy time for your family."

"But today seemed like such a better choice? Is that why you slept with me last night, because you thought it would make things easier for you and your family?"

Natalie jerked as if he'd slapped her. "No, of course not."

"You stayed under our roof, laughed with my dad, let us think you were just here for a friendly visit. God, I knew something wasn't right. All those times when you seemed as if you were somewhere else, you were just thinking of some way to spill the beans. Hell, why even tell us when you could have gotten off scot-free?"

Her heart felt as if it'd taken several hard punches from a boxer. "Scot-free? I didn't do anything other than not know how to tell you all the truth. Who the hell gets any training on how to tell the family of her childhood best friend that her drunk of a father killed the person who meant the most to them?"

"You had plenty of time to think about it."

The tears in Natalie's eyes spilled over, and she wiped them away with angry swipes. "Days during which I was mourning my father. He wasn't perfect by any stretch, but he was my dad and I loved him."

"You're telling me that you didn't know all these years, that you didn't wonder why your dad uprooted you out of the blue and made you move to another state?"

"I was a kid, one who was used to things

not going the way we wanted because my dad couldn't beat the bottle."

Fear welled up inside Natalie at the thought that Garrett and his family might go after her mother. Yes, her mom had kept a horrible secret for more than twenty years, but everything the woman had ever done was to help keep their family from falling apart.

Garrett stalked away several steps, rubbing his hand down over his face.

"I'm so—"

"Don't. Just don't. I don't want to hear it." He turned his head toward her. "You've said and done enough."

Her heart broke as he strode from the barn, pulled himself up into the saddle and kicked his horse into a full gallop. She listened to the pounding hooves until her quivering chin and blurry eyes dissolved into uncontrollable sobs. She wanted to scream at her father until she lost her voice. Even though he was gone, that one decision to drive drunk was still hurting people, her included.

Maybe she was just as big a fool as he'd been, though in a different way. He'd let alcohol control him. For her, it was her loneliness and love for Garrett and his family that was calling the shots. But she felt as if she'd made just as many bad decisions as her father.

Garrett's reaction to the truth kept playing over and over in her head, causing fresh waves of tears. It might make her a coward, but she couldn't face going through it again with Chloe, Wayne or even Owen. Though she couldn't drive, didn't even have her car, she couldn't stay on the ranch a minute longer. Though she was aware it was insane and that she was running away just as her father had, she got to her feet and made her way toward the road at the end of the driveway. If she had to walk all the way to Blue Falls on her crutches, she would. She was leaving the Brodys alone, as she should have done in the first place.

Chapter Twelve

Garrett wasn't aware of how long he'd ridden when he finally pulled his horse to a stop because he couldn't see past his tears. He couldn't remember the last time he'd cried, but Natalie's revelation had dredged up all the gut-wrenching memories of his mother's death and the hard years that had followed. And all that time the killer had been someone they knew.

God, he'd never wanted to punch something so much in his life. The horse sensed his mood and sidestepped nervously. Before his blind rage caused him to do something to hurt the animal, he dismounted and left the horse to graze while he stalked up the hill. When he reached the top, he stared out across the land that meant so much to him. The land his mother had loved every bit as much as his dad did. The same land he'd shown Natalie the day he'd first kissed her.

She'd used him, softened him up before spewing forth her awful truth. What a fool he'd been. How had he not seen that her supposed attraction for him was just an act? He hated himself that the loss of Natalie hurt as much as the words she'd spoken. Damn, he felt cursed.

He reached down and picked up a rock then drew back and threw it as far as he could, yelling as he did so. Then came another, and another. He threw and let his anger and pain echo across the pasture until his arm muscles burned and he collapsed onto his knees.

In that moment, he became the little boy he'd been all those years ago when his father had told him, Owen and Chloe that their mother was gone and she wasn't coming back. He could still see the haunted look on his father's face as if it had been only the night before and not a night two decades ago.

He tried to remember Natalie's father, but only bits of memories surfaced. How could he have lived all those years knowing he'd killed someone? Did he even care? Or was he too drunk to remember until he was dying and trying to make things right before he met his judgment?

Garrett's fingers dug into his palms, and he stared up at the sky so he wouldn't cry anymore. He had to pull himself together and figure out how he was going to tell his father the truth. He hated Natalie for putting him in the position to have to tarnish these early days of his siblings' marriages. And he couldn't stand the idea of his dad reliving that loss. Part of him wished Natalie had stayed in Kansas along with her promise to be the bearer of her father's too-late confession. He ground his teeth as he thought that her father had once again taken the coward's way out, confessing his crime only when he couldn't be made to pay for it.

And Garrett wanted someone to pay for it.

Needing to be alone with the decisions he had to make, he took the opportunity to ride part of the fence line though he'd done so only a few days earlier. He lost track of time as his thoughts continued to swirl like a spring tornado. But when he considered that Natalie might talk to his dad, too, he turned his horse around and headed for home.

When he arrived at the house, it was to find that not only was his dad there but so were Owen and Linnea, Chloe and Wyatt. His heart started beating faster as he didn't even take the time to return his horse to the barn, instead tying the reins to one of the porch supports at the front of the house. Fear that Natalie was dropping the bomb on the rest of his family propelled him up the steps and into the house.

The sound of laughter stopped him just inside the door. And the sight of the two sets of newlyweds, all smiles, hit him so hard that he wanted to turn around and hide in the barn for the foreseeable future. The truth was he was pretty sure he'd fallen in love with Natalie faster than he would have ever imagined possible. The idea that maybe it had all been a lie was eating him up inside.

"Hey, there you are," Chloe said when she spotted him just outside the doorway to the kitchen. "You pull a lone-cowboy-on-the-range deal today?"

"Something like that." He scanned the room but didn't see Natalie. If she was hiding in the guest room and everyone out here seemed to be in good spirits, he still had the choice of whether or not to tell them about the circumstances surrounding his mom's death.

"What's wrong?"

He met his dad's gaze and had his answer. The truth had been hidden long enough. "I need to tell you all something, and it's not going to be easy to hear." He let his eyes meet those of everyone around the table. "Natalie told me why she came back to Blue Falls." He paused, took a deep breath then focused on his dad. "Her dad was the one who crashed into Mom that night. He was…he was the one who killed her."

Chloe and Linnea gasped, and he sensed more than saw his brother-in-law and brother pull them into their arms. But Garrett kept his gaze on his dad, who looked as if he'd taken a jolt from a cattle prod to his heart.

"Are you sure?" Chloe asked, drawing his attention away from his dad.

"Yes. She hid it from us all this time." He told them everything Natalie had said, whether he believed it or not.

"Where is she?" His dad's voice sounded shaky and…older.

"The last time I saw her was in the barn, but that was hours ago."

His dad got slowly to his feet and headed for the back door.

"Dad?"

The man who had raised them on his own just shook his head once, saying without words that he needed to be alone. That or he was going to find Natalie and face her himself. For several seconds after his dad stepped outside, nobody moved or said anything. But then a rush of rage welled up in Garrett. He grabbed a coffee mug from the counter beside him and threw it across the room, causing it to shatter against the far wall.

After a few more seconds, Owen was the first to speak. "What did you say to Natalie when she told you?"

"That I didn't appreciate being used because she thought it would be easier to break the news afterward."

The faces staring back at him winced.

"Oh, Garrett, you didn't," Chloe said.

What the hell was wrong with them? "Why are you reacting this way? She lied to all of us, pretending to be our friend before lowering the boom."

Though his sister's eyes were shiny with tears, her innate sense of trying to see the good in people shone through. But she was wrong this time.

"What her father did was awful, but it wasn't her fault. She was a victim as much as we were."

"How can you say that? She's been here for days and didn't say a word."

"Days during which she saved my horse, helped out Doc Franklin and was repaid for her kindness by being trampled by a bull. How easy do you think it was for her to come here?"

He wished Chloe would stop taking Natalie's side. He wanted someone to be as angry as he was. But then, none of them had been on the verge of giving her their heart.

Garrett paced across the width of the kitchen. "We would have been better off if she'd never come here." He made the mistake of looking at Chloe. Her expression told him that she knew the real reason he was so angry—because he'd allowed himself to care for Natalie more than he'd ever cared for a woman before.

As they all fell into stunned silence, thunder rumbled in the distance. The sound was still fading when his dad came back inside.

"Is Natalie in her room?"

Surely she hadn't been in there listening to

the conversation going on out here. Anger at her still roiled within him even though a part of his heart wanted to let his sister's words ease that anger. He wondered if Natalie was too afraid to come out of the room. And why wouldn't she be after how he'd responded to her news? If she heard dishes crashing?

Damn, why were his feelings so twisted into knots?

Linnea hopped up from the table. "I'll check."

Garrett fought the urge to retreat outside. He wasn't entirely sure what he was going to feel or say if he looked into Natalie's eyes again. He couldn't just erase the anger and sense of betrayal. They'd cut too deep.

Linnea returned to the kitchen with a look of concern on her face. "She's not in there. Has anyone seen her since Garrett did earlier?"

Despite how mad he was, unease crept into his middle with all the other emotions when everyone indicated they hadn't seen Natalie all day.

"She's probably just sitting outside some-where," Chloe said as she stood. "Sometimes it's easier to think without four walls closing in on you."

"From the sound of that thunder, though, she needs to come inside," Linnea said.

They all headed outside and spread out in dif-ferent directions, calling out Natalie's name. Garrett hoped someone else found her because he wasn't ready to talk to her again, might never be. After several minutes, all of them made their way back to the front of the house. Garrett's concern grew at the expressions star-ing back at him. They all said something was wrong. Suddenly, the need to find Natalie safe and sound eclipsed all the other mixed-up feel-ings bombarding him.

"You think she headed into town?" Wyatt asked.

Garrett shook his head, wanting to believe that Natalie was just sitting somewhere out in the dark nearby, hiding from him and his anger. Just because he was upset with her didn't mean he wanted her physically hurt again.

"Her car's still in town, and she can't drive with that cast anyway," he said.

"She could have hitched a ride," Owen said.

Linnea shook her head. "But all her stuff is still here. And she wouldn't have left Milo behind. I've never seen someone fall in love with a dog so fast."

Was it possible she had fallen in love with him that quickly, too? Despite his accusation, had what they shared the night before been real?

His gaze caught Chloe's.

"Do you think she was upset enough to just start walking?"

"On crutches?" Owen said. "That's too far. She'd never make it."

"If you're upset enough, you don't think rationally," Chloe said.

Details of their heated conversation came back to him. If he peeled away his anger and let himself believe she hadn't meant to hurt him or his family, he could see the look in her eyes right before he'd stormed off. He hadn't been the only one in pain.

Garrett looked toward the roadway now cloaked in darkness. What if she had set out on foot? How far would she get before she couldn't go any farther? What if someone had picked her up, someone bad? Worst-case scenarios started flying through his head.

A fresh wave of anger built that she was now making him worry about her, the woman who had shattered the happiness his family had managed to find. But he couldn't help thinking that if something happened to her, it would be his fault.

He had to find her. Once he was sure she was safe, he could wrap himself in his anger again, return to trying to figure out if there was any way he could forgive her. If she deserved forgiveness.

He grabbed his phone and walked away from the group. But when he asked for Natalie at the Country Vista Inn this time, the clerk responded that they didn't have a guest by that name but that the car he described was still parked at the edge of the lot. His stomach sank even further as he turned back toward the others. He could tell from the expressions on their faces that they were as worried as he was.

"Lin, you stay here in case she comes back," he said. "Wyatt, keep checking around here. I'll head to town."

"I'm coming with you," Chloe said.

"Dad and I will drive the other direction," Owen said.

Panic beginning to take root inside him, Garrett raced to his truck as rain started to fall. Chloe hopped in beside him.

"We'll find her," she said.

He wasn't sure if she was trying to convince him or herself.

As he pulled onto the road and headed toward Blue Falls, the heavens opened up with an ill-timed deluge. Even with the windshield wipers on their fastest setting, it was hard to see the road. He drove slowly, not wanting to slip off the side or hit Natalie if, God forbid, she was out in this mess.

"Would she really try to walk?" he asked out loud. "That would be insane."

"Having your heart broken can make you do crazy things you'd never normally do."

He glanced over at her. "You think I broke her heart?"

"Now's not the time to talk about this."

"No, I want to know." But he refocused on the road, hoping it would provide some sort of buffer or distance between him and his sister's words.

Chloe sighed. "No matter what he did, she's mourning her father." She paused. "And her feelings for you are as obvious as the fact that it's raining. You'll think I'm nuts, but it feels like one of those meant-to-be sort of things. I mean, she had the biggest crush on you when we were kids."

He jerked his gaze toward her again. "She did?"

"Don't tell me you had no idea."

"I didn't."

"We've really got to work on your sense of awareness."

Evidently.

He cursed the rain and the way it restricted his view. He leaned forward over the steering wheel. The wipers swiped the windshield in front of him in time for him to notice something silver on the side of the road. He hit the brakes when he realized it was an aluminum crutch.

"God, no," he said as he threw the truck into Park and jumped out into the rain. His heart in his throat, he called out, "Natalie! Natalie, where are you?"

He grabbed the crutch and looked up and down the road. When he saw no sign of her, he peered into the darkness along the side of the road, praying she hadn't been hit by a car and was lying dead in the ditch.

Because of him.

Chloe ran up next to him, a flashlight in hand. She shined it into the ditch, which was already flowing with a river of murky water. They both called out Natalie's name. He would never forgive himself if she was hurt or worse. Damn it, why couldn't he be as understanding as his sister? Why had he stormed off instead of listening to Natalie? He hadn't given the first thought to how gut-wrenching it must have been for her when she found out what her father had done. He remembered enough about her younger self to know she'd cared for his mother a great deal. She'd cried over her passing every bit as much as Chloe had. But he'd forgotten that in the hot rush of anger and renewed sorrow.

"Stop," he said, holding out his arm toward Chloe. He strained to hear anything other than the pounding rain. Then there it was, a distinctly human sound. "Natalie!"

He hurried up the side of the road, desperate to find her. The beam of the flashlight finally illuminated her clinging to a flimsy-looking sapling growing out of the side of the embankment. One look at her drawn face, and he knew she couldn't hang on much longer. He couldn't let her be swept away in a flash flood. He saw her lips move, but no sound emerged. At least nothing he could hear.

Her fingers slipped, and Garrett launched himself into the waist-deep water. Horror filled him as he watched the fight go out of her eyes and her desperate grip failed her. As the water tugged at him and tried to steal her away, he grabbed her wrist and pulled with all his strength. He slipped and nearly went under himself, but he fought until he could grab the end of the crutch Chloe was holding out to him. Gradually, he pulled Natalie free of the water, pushing her up the bank toward Chloe.

"Come on," his sister called out over the sound of the storm as she clutched Natalie with one hand and held out the crutch with the other.

"I'm fine," he said, struggling to make himself heard. "Take her."

Chloe grabbed under Natalie's arms and

dragged her up to the road. Garrett didn't even take time to fully catch his breath as he followed on his hands and knees. He sucked in great gulps of air as Natalie coughed up muddy water.

"We've got to get her to the hospital," Chloe said in her doctor voice.

Though all of his muscles felt like overcooked noodles, he scooped Natalie up into his arms and headed for the passenger side of the truck. Chloe hopped into the driver's seat and headed toward town. He pulled the blanket he and Natalie had shared the night before from the back and wrapped it around her cold, soaked body. And tried not to think about the last time he'd held her in his arms. He rubbed her exposed flesh, scared to find it so icy. How long had she been in the water? God, how long had she been in the ditch? Why hadn't anyone seen the crutch and stopped to investigate?

She tried to say something, but it came out a garbled mess.

"Shh," he said. "We've got you. You're safe now."

Despite his best efforts to warm her up, she was still shivering when Chloe pulled up to the emergency room door at the hospital. As he carried Natalie inside, Chloe started calling out orders to the nurses on duty.

When another doctor met them and Natalie was suddenly being taken from his arms, he didn't want to let her go. Despite how he'd pushed her and her explanations away that morning, now he was afraid to let her out of his sight.

Chloe took his hand and squeezed to draw his attention from where Natalie was being wheeled to an examination room.

"I promise we'll take good care of her."

He saw in her eyes the knowledge of how

he felt about Natalie, feelings that prevented him from sitting down when his sister disappeared into the exam area. That mass of confused feelings had him pacing a trench in the floor and berating himself for pushing Natalie to the point where she'd nearly gotten herself killed.

He had no idea how they would deal with the truth of how her dad had nearly destroyed Garrett's family, but right now that wasn't his main concern. As the rain continued to come down in sheets outside, all that mattered was that they'd found Natalie in time. And that she had to be okay.

NATALIE RECOGNIZED THE sounds and smells of the hospital even before she opened her eyes. She wasn't in that ditch, cold, soaked to the bone and trying not to drown anymore. Just the memory of feeling helpless, and the foolish decision that had led to her being in that situation, sent a shiver through her body. As she moved to pull her blanket up over her arms, someone leaned forward in the chair beside her bed.

"You're awake."

As soon as Natalie saw Wayne, she could tell he knew about her dad. Tears filled her eyes. Unable to stop them, they overflowed to trail down her cheeks. "I'm so sorry," she said, her voice raw from screaming for help. Screams that she had feared would go unheard, until miraculously Garrett had found her.

No, she couldn't think about him.

To her utter surprise, Wayne took her hand between his two warm, work-roughened ones. "Shh, no tears. It wasn't your fault."

"The fact I didn't tell you immediately upon my arrival is."

"You were put in an unfair situation." He

looked down at their joined hands. "But I want you to tell me everything."

"Didn't Garrett tell you?"

"I suspect he didn't give you time to fully explain."

She bit her bottom lip before asking, "Are you sure you want to hear this?"

He lifted his gaze to hers. "No, but I need to. I've lived all these years with a hole in my heart where Karen should have been, and I didn't even know why she was gone."

She closed her eyes and wondered when the pain would stop. If it ever would.

"If you need to wait until you feel better—"

"No," she said. "You've waited long enough." She repeated everything she'd told Garrett and continued with what she'd aimed to tell him before his hasty exit prevented it. "It's okay if you're angry. I'm still angry. But even though it might not make any difference, I do believe he was genuinely sorry for what he did. I know that doesn't change anything, but...I needed you to know that. It's up to you whether you read it, but there is a letter from him to you in my bag at the house."

Wayne didn't react for several seconds and then just gave a slight nod. After another stretch of silence, he lifted his tear-filled eyes. "Thank you for telling me. I know it was hard."

She blinked fresh tears away. "I loved her, too, as much as my own mom."

"I know you did. And she loved you."

Natalie grabbed one of the rough tissues from the box sitting on the rolling table on the other side of the bed and dabbed her eyes.

Wayne stood and leaned over her. His kiss on her forehead was almost her total undoing.

"I'm glad you're okay," he said. "You had us all scared half to death, especially Garrett."

She shook her head. "I appreciate you saying

that, but I know Garrett hates me. And I understand. There's a part of me that hates myself."

Wayne started to say something, but then stopped. Was he realizing that she was right? Her heart broke even more at that thought.

After a few moments, he said, "Give him time. This was a shock."

Natalie managed to nod, but she knew the brief time she'd had with Garrett was over.

Wayne squeezed her hand. "Feel better." And then he walked out of the room, his boots clunking on the tile as he retreated down the corridor toward the exit.

She'd give anything if she could follow him out that door and leave this latest blast of heartache behind. Instead, she turned her back on the door and stared at the wall filled with posters about patient safety and the dry-erase board that identified today's nurse as Ginnifer. She tried to distract herself by reading all of the posters, but they blurred as her eyes filled with tears again.

She had to find a way to get out of this hospital and out of Blue Falls without seeing Garrett again. She couldn't face him when she knew in her heart that she loved him and he didn't love her back. Her decision to keep the truth from his family had killed any hope of him reciprocating her feelings. And that she couldn't blame on her father. Her heartache was of her own making.

Chapter Thirteen

Garrett released the jack, allowing the truck to lower back to the ground. He eyed the spare, already detailing in his mind the next ten tasks on his to-do list. It didn't matter that he hadn't slept the night before or that he'd been working since about two in the morning. He had to keep busy, occupy his mind with anything and everything but Natalie and the horrible revelation that her father had killed his mother. If he slowed down for even a moment, he started imagining that night, wondering if his mom had seen the other vehicle coming. The official report said that she'd died instantly, but was that true? Had she even for a moment looked into the eyes of the man who'd killed her?

He hadn't wondered about those kinds of details in a long time, not until Natalie had conveyed her father's confession. Why? Why did it have to be her father? Why when he'd finally found someone he could imagine spending his life with?

Burning, visceral anger welled up within him. Without thinking, he drew back and punched the truck. Pain shot up his arm, but he didn't care.

"That's not the wisest way to deal with your anger."

He'd been so wrapped up in his own swirling thoughts that he hadn't heard Chloe come out of the house. She'd arrived early that morning, most likely to talk to their dad. "You deal in your way. I'll deal in mine."

As was typical with his sister, she didn't let the conversation drop. Instead, she walked up beside him and leaned back against the driver's-side door of the truck.

"You disappeared last night."

"I heard Natalie was fine, so there was no reason for me to stay."

"I don't think that's true. You obviously care about her."

He didn't plan to respond, but for some reason the words tumbled out anyway. "I thought I did."

Chloe sighed. "I know you think she used you, but that's also not true. I talked to her last night. She just didn't know how to tell you, how to tell any of us."

"Sounds like a convenient excuse."

"Garrett, don't be so hard on her."

He met Chloe's gaze. "How would you feel if Wyatt told you out of the blue that his father killed Mom?"

Chloe flinched, and for a moment he was

sorry. But he needed to make her understand why he couldn't just forgive and forget. Even if Natalie truly hadn't known about what her father had done until he was on his deathbed, she'd still had a lot of opportunities to tell him before he'd gotten so wrapped up in her. And she hadn't.

"I imagine it would be every bit as hard for him to confess that as it was for Natalie. You don't honestly believe she came here with the intent to hurt us, do you? When it would have been so much easier to just promise her father she'd tell us and then not follow through?"

Garrett clenched his fist despite how it made it hurt even more. "Maybe you're just a more forgiving person than I am."

"Why don't you talk to her? And really listen this time. She's being dismissed today. You could go pick her up."

He shook his head. "I can't."

Before she could badger him even more, he strode toward the barn. Once inside the cooler interior, he fought the urge to punch something else. Instead he walked up to the wall of the tack room and leaned his forehead against the rough wood. He wished he knew what to do with all the anger trying to choke the life from him. And why all twisted up with the anger was the profound relief he'd felt the night before when a nurse had come out and told him that Natalie was going to be fine. He'd had the urge to scream and cry at the same time, and he'd fled the ER waiting room despite his dad and brother calling out to him.

How was it possible to have two totally opposite feelings toward a person at the same time? As he thought about Natalie, part of him wanted to yell at her until he lost his voice. But he couldn't deny that beneath that suffocating layer of anger was the desire to pull her into his arms and tell her everything was okay.

But it wasn't.

AS THE DAY wore on, Natalie's mind continued to war with itself. One minute, she hoped the footsteps nearing her door belonged to Garrett. The next, she told herself it was best if he continued to stay away, that it would be easier if she never saw him again.

She wasn't very good at lying to herself. Nothing about this situation was easy.

When the doctor finally released her, after all the paperwork and getting dressed that came with being dismissed, part of her wanted desperately for Garrett to pick her up so they could talk, at least say goodbye without harsh words. But it wasn't Garrett who stepped into her room.

"Hey there," Chloe said. "You look better than

the last time I saw you." She patted the cast on Natalie's leg. "I see you got a new model."

Natalie swallowed her disappointment. "Yeah, evidently going impromptu ditch swimming isn't good for a cast."

"You ready to blow this joint?"

"Yes. If I never see the inside of a hospital again, it'll be too soon."

When they reached the parking lot, Natalie scanned the surrounding area.

"I'm sorry he hasn't come to see you, but I told Garrett I wanted to pick you up." Natalie wasn't sure that last part was true, but she didn't question her friend. She just counted herself lucky that at least Chloe was still speaking to her, even after they'd had a long discussion late the night before about the parents they'd lost and why.

Chloe opened the passenger door of her car and helped Natalie maneuver into the seat.

"It's okay." Natalie said the words as her heart sank. But what was she expecting, Garrett to be waiting for her with open arms? Despite the fact that he'd saved her, had shown concern, she couldn't believe everything was okay just because she'd fallen in a ditch.

Chloe crouched next to Natalie. "He cares about you. I'm pretty sure that he loves you."

Natalie shook her head. "You're wrong."

"I know my brother pretty well, and you didn't see his face when he spotted you hanging on in that water."

"He would have helped anyone in the same situation."

"You're right. He would have because he's a good guy. But he wouldn't have had the look of abject terror on his face that I saw when he realized the danger you were in."

Natalie took a deep breath and stared at her

hands as she picked her cuticles. "There's just too much standing between us."

"There doesn't have to be. What happened wasn't your fault, and deep down Garrett knows that. We all do."

Natalie lifted her gaze to her friend's. "How could he ever look at me and not remember what my dad did?"

"Tell me this. What do you see when you look at Garrett?"

Every moment they'd shared since her return to Blue Falls rushed through her memory like a movie on fast-forward. "Someone who deserves to be happy."

"And you don't think you could be the person who makes him happy. I'd say your date the other night says otherwise."

"He told you about that?"

"No, but Dad said you two came in pretty

late. And I know there's not a single place open in Blue Falls at that hour."

Natalie's cheeks heated, causing Chloe to smile.

"But that was before he knew about my dad, and it shouldn't have been."

Chloe placed her hand on Natalie's knee just above the cast. "None of us knows what we would have done in the same situation. But when you care about someone like I think you care about Garrett, emotions shove logic and our best intentions off the nearest cliff."

Natalie tried to believe there was a future for her and Garrett, but she just couldn't see it no matter how much she wanted to be with him. Some things simply weren't meant to be.

"Maybe it's not Garrett's forgiveness you need," Chloe said.

As those words sank into Natalie's brain like water through cracks, she thought that perhaps her friend was right. Unless she could overcome her own feelings of guilt and believe in a future for her and Garrett, there wouldn't be one even if he decided he wanted one.

"I need to go home," Natalie said.

"I know." Chloe sounded as if that made her sad. "But I hope it's only temporary."

Natalie wasn't sure how she felt about that. She had a home, a life and her mother in Wichita. She couldn't just abandon her mother now that Natalie's dad was gone. Besides, no matter how much she loved Blue Falls, the Brody family and the idea of taking over Dr. Franklin's practice, there was no way she'd be able to see Garrett around town and get over him.

Chloe gave her a friendly squeeze on the knee before standing and shutting the door. During the entire ride back to the Brodys' ranch, Natalie yearned for some clear path to present itself. Because right now she had no idea what to do, what to believe, even what to hope for.

GARRETT TENSED WHEN he heard Chloe's car turning into the driveway. By the time she parked, he was so knotted up inside that he had to talk himself out of walking out of the back of the barn and away from the main part of the ranch.

"Garrett!"

He closed his eyes and took a deep breath before heeding his sister's call and making his way to the entrance to the barn.

Chloe motioned for him to come toward the car. Damn it, he should have known she wouldn't give up so easily and let him keep his distance from Natalie.

When he reached the car, he opened the passenger door. But Natalie didn't immediately move to get out. When Chloe pulled crutches out of the backseat, he glanced across at her. The look she gave him said to be gentle, to say something instead of standing there like a fence post.

Finally, Natalie shifted her legs out of the car and allowed him to help her to her feet.

The silence between them felt so strained that he searched for something to say to fill it.

"How are you feeling?" He found he truly wanted to know.

"Tired." She didn't meet his eyes, and he found himself wondering what she was thinking.

"You want to lie down?" An unwanted rush of warmth hit him as he remembered how he'd picked her up and carried her up the front steps, how she'd felt in his arms.

She glanced toward the house as Chloe handed her the crutches then returned to the back of the car to retrieve a small bag and a bakery box. "I think I'll stay outside for a while. The sun feels good."

He wondered if she was still reliving how cold she'd been when he'd pulled her out of the water. He didn't like to think about it, but if she wanted to sit in the sun until it sank over the horizon that made perfect sense.

She didn't head for the porch but rather the corral, where Owen was working with his latest horse purchase.

Garrett knew he should return to work in the barn, but when he looked around, Chloe was already halfway up the front steps. Despite his decision to steer clear of Natalie, he wasn't willing to leave her alone, not with how pale and shaky she looked.

"That's a pretty animal," she said as she reached a stack of hay bales they'd placed outside the corral so potential buyers could watch Owen work the horses.

"Yeah. Turns out my little brother is really good at training horses."

A small smile tugged at her lips. "Who'd have thought the brat who used to attack Chloe and me with water balloons would grow up to be so…grown-up."

After she seated herself, he hesitated before climbing up beside her. He resisted the urge to entwine his fingers with hers. The quiet that followed made him squirm.

"Are you doing okay?" he finally asked.

"I've been better, but I'll manage."

He wondered how many times she'd had that thought in her life.

She watched Owen and the horse for a couple of minutes then turned slightly toward Garrett. "I'm truly sorry, for everything, from the bottom of my heart."

At first, he wanted to flee from the conversation, but avoidance hadn't really helped, had it? Chloe's words came back to him. "I know."

"As soon as I'm able to make arrangements, I'm going home, back to work, my mom and my life."

Part of him wanted to tell her she could have a life in Blue Falls, but he wasn't sure that was true, no matter how much he cared for her. He doubted anything he said would matter anyway. Her weak smile told him that her mind was made up.

"I care about you, Garrett. I hope you know that. I wouldn't have shared the other night with you if I didn't. But I know I messed up, ruined everything."

He wanted to tell her that maybe they could find a way to be together, but the words wouldn't come.

"And I've got to deal with all this pain and anger and confusion," she said. "It feels as if they will choke the life out of me sometimes." She stopped and took a breath. "My dad wasn't good at responsibility, so I refuse to shirk mine."

Why couldn't he say something?

Natalie surprised him when she reached up and placed her palm against the side of his face. "You're a wonderful man, Garrett. I hope that you have the life you deserve."

"That makes it sound as if we'll never see you again." Wasn't that what he'd tried to convince himself he wanted?

"Maybe that's for the best."

He wanted to beg her to not go, but he wouldn't. She was probably right, and he had to accept that. No matter how much his heart was screaming at him not to give her up.

With a final sad smile, she slid off the hay bales and headed toward the house. No doubt to pack up her things and leave his family behind again, this time for good.

"HOW'S SHE DOING?" Garrett asked when he stepped into the barn several days later to find Chloe checking on Penelope's wound.

"Healing up nicely. Natalie did a great job with her."

The pang in his chest at the sound of Natalie's name propelled him toward the tack room. He wondered how long it was going to take to get over her. Shouldn't it be easier to do considering everything that had happened? How he'd told himself it would never work, that he'd never be able to look at her without remembering how she'd made love to him while keeping secret the reason for her visit. But she'd been gone a week thanks to a friend flying down and driving her back in her car, and he hadn't stopped thinking about her yet. No matter how many times he tried to tell himself that the next day would be easier, it never was.

Chloe followed him and blocked his way out

of the tack room. "So, you're not going to go after her?"

"No. Why would I?"

"Because you love her. And loving someone doesn't mean the road is always easy. Sometimes it's hard, but you work through it together."

He could deny he cared about Natalie, but Chloe would know he was lying. "Sometimes loving someone isn't enough."

"Bull."

"Chloe, I know you're trying to help, but you need to let this go. Besides, Natalie has a life in Kansas."

Chloe rolled her eyes. "I swear men are so incredibly dense sometimes."

"Do I dare ask?"

"Of course she went home. You didn't give her a reason to stay."

"Do you really think it would ever work?"

"Yes, if you'd tell her you love her, you idiot.

Make her believe in the depths of her heart that what her father did doesn't change that."

As he went about his work the rest of the morning, he couldn't stop thinking about what Chloe said. Was he strong enough to let go of his lingering doubts, the last remnants of the pain Natalie's revelation had caused? And what if he risked baring his soul only to find out she didn't feel the same?

But something told him that she did, that she was standing in her own way of happiness the same as he was. He wasn't a big-gesture kind of guy, but by the end of the day he'd decided that it was Owen's turn to work double duty while he made a trip to Kansas.

Before he did anything, though, he needed to talk to his dad.

After they finished dinner that night and his dad started to get up from the table, Garrett stopped him. "I need to ask you something."

"This have anything to do with Natalie?"

"Yes. I need to know if having her here would be too difficult for you."

"Not near as difficult as seeing my oldest son let the woman he loves slip through his fingers. Trust me when I say that when you find the woman who makes your heart beat so fast you'd swear your chest can't contain it, you grab on and don't let go."

"But what about—"

"Don't worry about me. It was a shock, yes. But after talking with her and reading her dad's letter, I'm working on coming to peace with it. And I will never hold it against Natalie. I loved that little girl like she was my own, and it didn't take long for that to come back."

Excitement started pumping through Garrett's veins. "Chloe thinks I should go after Natalie."

His dad smiled. "Your sister always was the smartest one of us."

Chapter Fourteen

"You look dog tired," said Ashley, who worked the front desk at the animal clinic, to Natalie at the end of the day.

"That's because I am." Even though she'd been home for a week, she felt every bit as wrung out as she had when she left Blue Falls. Her injuries still caused her some pain, her apartment felt incredibly empty even with the addition of Milo, and she missed Garrett so much that sometimes she thought her heart might turn to dust and blow away across the prairie.

Dr. Jasper, the head vet, walked out of his office and met Natalie's gaze. "When will you be out of your cast?"

She'd always known he was a no-nonsense kind of guy, but it had never rubbed her the wrong way before. Now it did, especially when she thought about how kind and affable Doc Franklin was with his animal patients, their human owners and his employees.

"About another month."

"Okay, we'll make do until then."

His tone got on her last nerve, and she made her way outside before she said something she'd regret. She didn't know what was wrong with her. First she left Blue Falls because it didn't feel right to stay. But now that she was home, it felt wrong here, too.

Maybe things would start getting better when she saw her mom in a few minutes. Thankfully, her mom had arrived back home from France the night before, and Natalie was actually looking forward to hearing about her adventures. The few pictures she'd seen Renee post online almost hadn't seemed real, but she'd detected a flicker of life in her mom's eyes she hadn't seen in a long time.

She sank onto the metal bench under the big tree out front to wait for her mom. At least now she wouldn't have to depend on friends and co-workers to tote her to work and back. But as the minutes ticked by and her mom didn't show, she wondered if the jet lag had her mom's schedule so messed up that she was sleeping. She pulled out her phone but then saw a familiar car turning the corner.

Her mom pulled her aging sedan to the curb and hopped out. "So sorry I'm late." She glanced at Natalie's cast. "Oh, honey."

"It's okay, really." She wasn't about to tell her mom that this was actually the second cast required for the same broken leg or about the events that had led to the need for a replacement cast.

Once they were both in the car, her mom didn't drive toward Natalie's apartment or her own house.

"Where are we going?"

"For ice cream. I've had a hankering for a giant milkshake all day."

They went to Dave's Drive-In and both ordered milkshakes. "This was a good idea, Mom."

"I brought Renee here when she broke her arm skating when she was in second grade."

"Oh, so it's the official broken-bone stop. Got it."

Her mom chuckled a little.

"It's nice to hear you laugh."

"It feels weird, like I shouldn't be able to."

"I know what you mean."

Her mom looked over at her, a touch of anxiety in her expression. "How did things go with the Brodys? I still can't believe your dad asked you to do that and that you agreed."

"It was rough at first."

"At first?"

"They're understandably upset, but we parted on friendly terms." At least as friendly as she could possibly expect. Not wanting to go into more detail, Natalie changed the topic. "What I want to know is how did you like Paris? The pictures made it look as if you were having a nice time."

"It was like being in a movie, as if it wasn't real. But I actually loved it. Does that make me a bad person?"

"Why on earth would you ask that?"

"Because I just lost your dad."

Natalie reached across the car and grabbed her mom's hand. "I know you loved him and miss him, but you missed out on a lot in life because you were so busy trying to keep our family together, fed and a roof over our heads. You deserve to do whatever you want now. You can cry when you need to and laugh when it feels right, all without any guilt. Most women would have left Dad long ago, but you stuck it out."

"He wasn't all bad."

"I know that. He just had a lot of demons he wasn't able to slay, and we were all collateral damage even if we loved him."

Her mom grew quiet.

"Is something else bothering you?" Natalie asked.

"The reason I was late today was because I was meeting with a real estate agent about selling the house."

Though that bit of news surprised Natalie, she could understand her mom not wanting to live in the same space she'd shared with Natalie's dad. It was hard to move on when you were constantly surrounded with reminders of your loss.

"I think that's a good idea. You could always get an apartment in my complex. There's usually a vacancy or two."

"Actually, I'm thinking about making a bigger change. Would you feel as if I'm abandoning you if I moved to Kansas City?"

Seemed it was a day for surprises. "Of course not. It makes sense you'd want to be close to the grandkids."

"This might sound crazy, but I'm thinking about splitting my time between staying with Allison and Renee. And of course I'll visit you, too."

"You're going back to Paris?"

"Yeah. I feel as if I only scratched the surface. Who knows? Maybe I'll even try to learn a little French."

Though it felt as if everything in Natalie's

world was falling apart, she couldn't help but smile. Though she knew her mom had loved her dad a great deal despite their less-than-easy life together, it was as if she was witnessing a rebirth. And her mom deserved it.

They talked more about her mom's plans as they headed to Natalie's apartment. Instead of dropping Natalie off, her mom parked but didn't make a move to get out of the car.

"I need to apologize to you," her mom said. "I should have been the one to tell the Brodys the truth."

"No, you shouldn't have." Natalie stunned even herself by saying that. "I think you'd borne enough guilt hiding Dad's secret all those years."

"But it wasn't right, even if we did it out of the fear of losing you girls. We ripped you from your home, away from your friends, and never told you why."

"What's done is done. Someone recently told me that maybe it's time to leave all the heartache in the past and move on, make new, happy memories."

"Sounds like a forgiving person." The way her mom said that sounded as if she'd guessed it was one of the Brodys.

"Yeah."

"Honey, is there something you haven't told me?"

"No. It's just that…the trip to Texas wasn't what I expected." She shook her head. "Listen, Mom. I'm pretty worn-out, so I'm going to go in and lie on my couch and pretend it's a nice bubble bath."

She thought at first her mom was going to question her further, but she didn't. Instead, she got out of the car and came around to help Natalie out.

"Thank goodness you're on the first floor."

Natalie adjusted her crutches, but before she could take the first step toward the sidewalk someone called her name. No, not just someone. She turned slowly toward the sound of his deep voice and couldn't believe her eyes.

"Garrett." Mixed in with the surprise in her voice was happiness to see him and fear for why he'd arrived on her doorstep when her mom was there. In her absence, had he decided that someone—her mother—had to pay for his mother's death?

Her mom gripped Natalie's arm, and when Natalie looked at her she saw the same fear in her mom's eyes.

Garrett took a few steps toward them and looked at Natalie's mom. "It's okay. I'm not here for the reason you think I am."

"You're not?" Her mom's voice sounded small and frightened, as if she was watching the new life she was planning for herself being snatched away before she could even begin living it. "Why are you here then?"

He took another step forward and Natalie tensed. That was in large part because of how much she ached to step into his arms and have him pull her close.

Instead of maintaining eye contact with her mother, he locked gazes with Natalie.

"For Natalie."

Not *to see* her.

Not *to talk to* her.

For her.

Natalie's heart sped up so much that she imagined the top story on that night's Wichita news being that the entire populace had heard a mysterious heart beating.

She sensed her mom staring at her. "What's going on?"

"I'm here to tell Natalie how I feel about her, something I should have done before she left.

And then I have to hope that's enough to convince her that Blue Falls is where she belongs, with me."

Natalie's knees went weak, but Garrett was there to steady her, just as he'd been so many other times.

Her mom took a step back and looked from Natalie to Garrett and back again. "I've definitely missed something."

"So have I," he said. "The fact that in only a few days, I fell totally in love with your daughter."

Natalie gasped and brought one hand up to her mouth. Garrett gently ran his hand along the side of her head, smoothing her hair, before cupping her jaw and rubbing his thumb across her cheek.

"I'm sorry that I was so unwilling to listen. And that I let you go because I thought that would be easier. But it wasn't, at least not for me. If you want to stay here, I'll respect that. But I had to tell you the truth. I love you, Natalie Todd. And I at least want to give us a chance."

Tears popped into her eyes as she let his words sink in.

"Is this really happening?"

She glanced at her mom, who looked every bit as shocked as Natalie felt.

"Yes," Garrett said, drawing her attention back to him. "I know it's not the most romantic place to confess my feelings. I'm risking looking like the world's biggest fool, but I didn't want to wait a moment longer."

She wanted to say yes, that she wanted the same thing with all her heart, but nothing had changed about the awful past that lay between their families. "How could this possibly work? When people find out about…" She paused and looked at her mom, not wanting to hurt her further despite the part she'd played in covering up the truth. Natalie shifted her gaze back to Garrett. "When they find out about what my dad did, they won't understand how you and your family can be around me."

"No one has to know but us."

"But the police?" her mom said, sounding as if she was surprised she'd spoken her biggest fear.

He looked at her mom. "It wouldn't change anything, so there's no need to tell them. I don't want to hang on to the past anymore. Neither does my family."

Her mom's sound of relief, as if twenty years of fear had just been alleviated, caused Natalie to pull her mom close for an embrace. After several moments, her mom stepped away.

Natalie met his gaze. Still half believing this was a dream and she would wake up any minute, she asked, "Are you sure?"

"Positive. I know that you have things tying you here. Your mom—"

"She's moving to Kansas City."

"And your job—"

"I can work anywhere there are animals."

"Then the only questions left to answer are do you feel the same way I do, and do you want to take a chance?"

As Natalie looked up at the face of the man she loved, everything that had been holding her back fell away, allowing her to breathe fully for the first time since her father's confession.

"Yes."

Garrett's eyes widened as if he'd been prepared for rejection. "Really?"

She laughed. "Yes, really. I love you, Garrett. I just didn't think you could love me."

He took her hand. "You aren't your father." He shifted his gaze to her mom. "And you aren't your husband." Again he looked at Natalie. "I won't say it doesn't hurt, because it does. But I don't think your dad was evil. I know he didn't do what he did on purpose."

A sob broke free from her mom, but Natalie couldn't move to hold her. She was too afraid that if she even blinked then everything that was happening would be revealed as a cruel dream taunting her with all she could ever want.

Garrett took Natalie's hands in his, not once breaking eye contact. "From this moment, I only want to look forward. With you."

"I love you," she said, her voice barely a whisper.

He smiled. "Then if your mom doesn't mind, I'm going to kiss you."

"Don't mind me," her mom said through her sniffles.

As Garrett gathered Natalie close and brought his lips to hers, she didn't think there was any possible way she could ever be happier than she was in that moment.

NATALIE LOCKED THE door of the clinic and looked up at the clear, blue October sky. She loved this time of year when the brutal heat of summer had lessened and the changing of seasons was in the air.

"Hi, Dr. Todd."

She looked toward the sidewalk in time to see little Sarah Thompson and her mom walking their German shepherd, Ernie.

"Hey," she said and waved. "Nice day for a walk."

As the mother and daughter continued up the street, Natalie couldn't help but smile. Though everyone was sad to see Dr. Franklin leave, the local pet owners and ranchers had welcomed her with a warmth that eased the nervousness that had accompanied her on her return trip to Blue Falls.

Even now, only weeks after she'd relocated, she still found it hard to believe how well things were going. She still woke up sometimes with her heart thundering, afraid it was all a dream and that Garrett hated her. It had even happened to her once when they'd spent the night together, and he'd pulled her into his arms and comforted her, telling her again that he could never hate her. That he hadn't even hated her in those horrible moments after she'd told him the truth about her dad. He'd been hurt, shocked, yes. But he hadn't hated her. He'd told her that it had hurt so much because he was already falling for her.

Though she knew it would take time to move past the pain they'd both endured, things were going remarkably well between them. A day didn't go by without her seeing him, sometimes only briefly because of their busy work schedules, but others when they were able to spend an entire day and night together. They went riding on the ranch, hiking at nearby parks, to dinner and movies in Austin, dancing at the music hall. They'd even driven down to San Antonio for a concert and a boat ride along the River Walk. Though she woke up each day thinking it was impossible to love him more, she was proven wrong.

Realizing she'd been standing in the same spot daydreaming for who knew how long, she headed for her truck. When she opened the door, a wide smile tugged at her mouth. Sitting in her seat was a bouquet of fall flowers full of vibrant orange lilies, burgundy daisies and happy yellow sunflowers. A folded piece of paper was propped against the flowers. Having no doubt whom it was from, Natalie grabbed the note and opened it.

Meet me at the cliff. I have a surprise for you.

It had been such a wonderful surprise to find out how much of a romantic Garrett Brody had hidden underneath that no-nonsense cowboy exterior. With excitement pumping in her veins, she slid into the truck and headed for the spot overlooking the lake where they'd first made love. They'd been back there a couple of times while out hiking, but something told her that Garrett wouldn't be so mysterious simply for another hike. Her blood heated as she considered she might be in for a repeat of that first night, only with a much better morning-after.

When she reached the parking lot at the bottom of the trail, she pulled in next to Garrett's truck then followed the path that led to the cliff overlooking the lake. She stopped and her heart filled with happiness when she saw the feast of a picnic Garrett had laid out on what she was pretty sure was the blanket they'd shared that night.

She shifted her gaze to Garrett, who was wearing a grin the size of Texas. She smiled back as she crossed to him.

"What's the occasion?"

"It's a beautiful day, and I felt like a picnic with a beautiful woman." He pulled her close and lowered his lips to hers.

After a couple of minutes of kissing, Natalie stepped back. "More of that later. Right now, I'm starving. I didn't have time for lunch."

"Any luck on finding someone else to join the practice?" he asked as they sat on the edge of the blanket.

"I've got a few possibilities. Just have to find the time to set up interviews."

"Lot different running your own show, huh?"

"Yeah."

"But you're loving it."

She smiled as she picked up a piece of cheese and a cracker. "I really am."

They chatted about the animals she'd tended that day, Owen's latest horse sale to an up-and-coming roper, and the news that they'd heard the night before, that Linnea was pregnant.

"Hard to believe how much has changed in

the past year," Garrett said before taking a bite of a chicken-salad sandwich.

Natalie slathered another cracker with the smoky cheese-and-pepper spread. "I think I could eat my weight in this stuff. Where did you get all this? Doesn't seem like Primrose fare."

"I might have hired Brooke Teague," he said, indicating Ryan Teague's wife and the chef out at the Teague family's guest ranch.

Natalie stopped with the cracker halfway to her mouth then set it back on her paper plate. "This is awfully fancy for a casual picnic."

Garrett turned in her direction and took one of her hands in his, rubbing his thumb across her skin, leaving a warm trail behind.

"That's because it's not a casual picnic."

Natalie's heart rate picked up, whether from excitement or anxiety she wasn't quite sure.

Sometimes the two danced a tango, making it hard to tell them apart.

"These weeks we've spent together since you came back have been the best of my life," he said.

"Mine, too."

"I know we agreed to go slow, and I will continue to do that if that's what you want. But I know what I want, and that's you."

She smiled. "I'm right here."

"Forever."

It took her a moment to realize that he was holding a white-frosted cupcake toward her. She blinked, not believing what she saw at first. But even after blinking, the diamond ring poking out of the icing was still there.

"Oh, Garrett."

"I love you," he said. "And I want nothing more than for you to be my wife."

She dragged her gaze away from the ring and looked him straight in the eye.

"Will you marry me, Natalie?"

Her heart beat even faster. "Are you sure?"

"Never been more sure of anything in my life."

"Then, yes, I will marry you."

He pulled her into his arms and kissed her as if to make sure she didn't change her mind.

When they finally ended the kiss, she watched with her heart beating like crazy as Garrett washed the frosting off the ring then slid it onto her finger. She placed her palm against the side of his face, finding it hard to believe she'd captured the heart of this cowboy. If he loved her even half as much as she loved him, then she was the luckiest woman alive.

Chapter Fifteen

Garrett couldn't stop fidgeting. He couldn't re-member ever having so much nervous energy flowing through his veins.

"Would you be still before you make me poke a hole in my finger?" Owen said from where he was trying to pin a boutonniere to Garrett's lapel.

"Sorry."

"Dude, I know how you're feeling, like you want to jump out of your skin. You just want to get all the pomp over with, but you go through it because it's important to women. They want this beautiful memory."

"I know. And Natalie deserves it."

"Yes, she does." Owen finished pinning and placed his hands atop his big brother's shoulders. "And so do you. I'm happy for you."

"Thanks."

A gentle knock on the door revealed itself to be that of Mrs. Todd. "Can I talk to you for a minute?"

"I'll wait for you outside," Owen said and left Garrett alone with the woman who would be his mother-in-law in a few minutes.

"Is everything okay?" he asked.

"Yes, fine. Natalie looks beautiful, though a little nervous."

"I know the feeling."

Mrs. Todd took a few more steps into his bedroom. "I just wanted to thank you for making Natalie so happy. She had to take on responsibility too young, and I've always felt guilty for that. Even though she wasn't a sad person and took everything in stride, I never realized how happy she could be until I saw her with you. And considering what brought you together, I count that as nothing less than a miracle."

Garrett crossed to her and took her hands in his. "You raised a wonderful daughter. If I bring her happiness, I'm glad. Because she couldn't make me any happier."

Though he knew he'd never forget the truth of what had happened to his mother, his decision to let the anger reside firmly in the past had freed him from a weight he hadn't realized he'd been carrying. And he had no doubt that his mom was looking down on him and smiling at his decision to move beyond her loss.

Because she looked as if she needed it, he pulled Natalie's mom into his arms and kissed her on top of her head. When she hugged him back, he imagined that his mom was there, as well. He closed his eyes and smiled.

I love you, Mom.

When Mrs. Todd stepped out of his embrace,

she squeezed his hands. "I hope you don't mind me saying so, but I feel as if I'm gaining a son I never had."

He squeezed her hands back. "I don't mind at all."

She gave a quick nod. "Well, I think the two of you have waited long enough, don't you?"

Yes, he did.

"IT'S SHOWTIME," CHLOE SAID.

Natalie's stomach rumbled in response.

"Someone is hungry," Renee said with a smile.

"If she's like I was when I got married," Allison said, "then she hasn't eaten a thing all day."

"Good thing there's quite the spread waiting for us," Chloe said. "I think Keri and Linnea have outdone themselves again."

"Watch out after the I-dos," Renee said. "She's likely to mow us all down to get to the buffet."

"Hello, right here," Natalie said.

They all laughed, which helped alleviate some of the tension knotted in Natalie's stomach like a ball of rubber bands.

Outside, music began to play at the same moment her mom returned from wherever she'd gone. Time to go get married to the love of her life.

Her friend and sisters led the way out the back to the white-cloth runner that wound around the side of the house toward the front steps, where Garrett had first swept her off her feet. The fresh spring air wafted through her veil, and she thought she couldn't have asked for a more beautiful day for her wedding.

"You ready?" her mom asked.

She was thankful for her mom at her side, giving her support. "Yeah."

Her heart thumped wildly as she rounded the corner and saw Garrett dressed in a dark suit with the bright orange rose pinned to his lapel.

But what filled her heart even more was how

his face transformed when he saw her. There was no doubt that he loved her, and that made her love him even more.

Chloe, Allison and Renee took their spots at the side of the steps opposite Owen, Wyatt and Simon Teague. Natalie glanced toward Wayne and was rewarded with a huge smile. When she and her mom reached the bottom of the steps, her mom kissed her cheek before handing her off to Garrett.

He took her hand. "Need me to carry you up the steps again?" he asked with a smile.

She smiled back. "Maybe later."

With two good, cast-free legs, she climbed the steps to stand beside the man who would soon be her husband. Even as the minister began the ceremony, she couldn't look away from Garrett. And he seemed to feel the same way.

She barely heard a word but somehow managed to respond at the appropriate points. But her hearing came back in time for her to hear,

"I now pronounce you husband and wife. You may kiss the bride."

Garrett did just that, and it wasn't a chaste peck on the lips. Taking a page out of his brother's and brother-in-law's books of mischief, he dipped her back across his arms and kissed her as if he'd been saving up for that kiss his entire life.

And maybe he had.

AS THE LAST of the wedding guests drove away from the ranch, Natalie looked out across the expanse of moonlit land. All those acres in the distance had such a rich family history, and she was a part of that history now. A part of the Brody family, of a community that had welcomed her with open arms—and a lot of business at the vet clinic.

"See any shooting stars?" Garrett asked as he stepped up behind her and wrapped his arms around her waist.

"No, but I don't need to." She turned to face him. "That day you proposed to me, I didn't think I could be any happier. I was wrong. I'm so happy right now that I feel as if I can't contain it all."

He leaned close. "Then maybe you should share some of it." When he waggled his eyebrows, she laughed.

"Are you volunteering?"

"Yes, ma'am."

And then he scooped her up in his arms and headed toward the house, which had been vacated for their wedding night.

"I can walk now, you know."

"Yeah, but I kind of like sweeping you off your feet."

She smiled as love filled every part of her. "I like it, too."

So she let him carry her toward the rest of their lives.

* * * * *